The Voyage of QV66

We know a lot about People. We don't know how long ago they went, or where they went to, but we know a great deal about them from the pictures of them everywhere, and from all the things they left behind – the things they used and the buildings they made and everything they had in their houses. Stanley looks and looks at pictures of the People. He says they give him the shivers (they give us all the shivers, as a matter of fact) but he feels kind of connected to them...

Penelope Lively

THE VOYAGE OF QV 66

Illustrated by Harold Jones

MAMMOTH

First published in Great Britain 1978
by William Heinemann Ltd
Reprinted 1979
Published 1990 by Mammoth
an imprint of Mandarin Paperbacks
Michelin House, 81 Fulham Road, London SW3 6RB
Reprinted 1990

Mandarin is an imprint of the Octopus Publishing Group

Text copyright © Penelope Lively 1978
Illustrations copyright © Harold Jones 1978

ISBN 0 7497 0360 1
A CIP catalogue record for this title is available
from the British Library

Printed in Great Britain
by Cox & Wyman Ltd, Reading

CONTENTS

For Adam, who helped in various ways

1

In which we meet the animals, especially Stanley, discover QV 66, and the voyage begins at Carlisle Station

I want to get the story told before we forget how it happened. We're beginning to, already. The trouble is, we're none of us very good at remembering; we have pictures in our heads, but we're not very clear about what came before what, or whether something happened a long time ago or just recently. And then Stanley starts making things up, and you don't know where you are any more.

It's hard to be certain now, even how we got together, the seven of us. Ned always says it was him. He says he found the boat and then hired the rest of us as crew, but of course that's nonsense. He's a good fellow, Ned, but he can get an idea in his head and then nothing in the world will dislodge it. Ned's a horse, I should add. He's always going on about his ancestors; he says one of them won something called a Derby, which was some kind of competition and this ancestor of his was best at it out of all the horses in the world. But then one day, during the voyage, we fetched up in the ruins of a town with a lot of factories and railways, and the sign on the road leading to it said DERBY, so obviously he was talking nonsense,

1

wasn't he? It was just a place. He says his name is Flying Warrior, too, which is ridiculous. We've always called him Ned.

But as I say, he's not a bad chap. We could never have made the voyage without him. At the beginning, when there was still a lot of water everywhere, he only had to pull the boat for short distances, in the high places, but later, when the water was going down, he had to do a lot of work. Freda helped, of course, but she made a fuss about it. She always said that's not what she's for. Freda's a cow.

Pansy's a cat. At least, she was a kitten when she first joined us, but she grew fast. We found her stuck up a tree when she was young; you couldn't help noticing her because she's bright orange with black and grey patches, and none of us had ever seen a cat like that before. So Stanley got her down and Freda insisted on adopting her. Freda is extremely sentimental; she's always finding young things and wanting to look after them. Once she tried to adopt a Shetland pony but it was a bad-tempered creature and kept kicking Ned, so we persuaded her to leave it behind and when we found Pansy we let Freda keep her instead, though I must admit that now Pansy is pretty well grown-up she and Freda aren't quite so attached.

I'm a dog, of course. My name's Pal. We know that because once when we were going over a rubbish tip somewhere we came across a tin that still had one of those paper pictures wrapped round it, and the picture was of me, and it had a name in big letters: PAL. I was tickled pink, I can tell you. The only thing is that a bit later we found another tin with a different picture of me and that was called CHUM, which got me all confused, because I like to know where I am about things and I can't manage more than one name at a time. So I stuck to Pal.

2

Offa is a pigeon. He was reared on the front of Lichfield Cathedral, on the right shoulder of a statue called King Offa, so as soon as he could read he took his name from that. He and I are the only ones who can read, and Stanley, of course. I'm never sure how I learned—just through being curious about the People and all their things, I suppose. Stanley just would, because he has to find out about everything. Offa says in his case it's the result of growing up in such elevated surroundings. As soon as he could fly he spent his time exploring the cathedral ruins and he's always reciting bits out of a big book that he says was chained up to a desk to the middle of the cathedral and that he learned by heart. Freda, Pansy and Ned can't read. Pansy's too lazy to learn, I reckon; Freda says it would be a bother and she's not very clever anyway and what's the point when there's always one of us to tell her what things say. Ned claims he's going to get around to it one of these days, when he's got some spare time, when we've finished traipsing around to oblige young Stanley there.

We didn't know what Stanley was then. He was the only one we'd ever seen. Everything used to stare at him. You could see he wasn't a dog or a cat or a bird, that was clear enough. What he looks most like, frankly, is People. But he's much smaller and he's got fur, and People didn't. We know now what Stanley is, of course, now that the voyage is finished, but I am going to tell things as they happened, in the proper order, so we will get to that in good time.

We know a lot about People. We don't know how long ago they went, or where they went to, but we know a great deal about them from the pictures of them everywhere, and from all the things they left behind—the things they used and the buildings they made and everything they had in their houses. We know what they looked like—that they didn't have fur or tails but they had hands and feet like Stanley does. Stanley looks and looks at pictures of the People. He says they give him the shivers (they give us all the shivers, as a matter of fact) but he feels kind of connected to them.

And we know that they were very clever, and very good at making things, and that there must have been a great many of them. Millions of them—many more than there are animals around now. You could say, I suppose, that we've not only spent a lot of time learning about them, but that we've learned a lot from them too. Not only how to do things, like working out the way they did something and then copying (as Stanley did with his tools—I'll get to that later) but the names they gave to everything. Everything they left behind—houses and factories and roads and cars and trains and books and rusty tins and broken bottles. Stanley knows most about that, of course, because of his extreme curiosity. He is always ferreting about amongst the People's buildings, picking up this and that, reading newspapers and labels and notices and books. "What's that?" Ned will say, offhand, kicking a broken-down metal thing with one wheel. "That's a wheelbarrow," Stanley will answer. "They put leaves in it and pushed it around, I saw a picture once." "What did they want to do that for, then?" Ned'll go on, and then Stanley shrugs and says, "*I* don't know. I don't often know *why* they did things. Just what they did."

As I've said, we don't know when they went, the People, but we suppose it must have been when the water came, and we think the water must have come very fast, because they went just like that, without taking much with them. Their stuff is everywhere. They seemed to need an amazing amount of different kinds of things—you

4

should see the insides of their houses, jammed full of this, that and the other. Of course, most of it is in a fair mess now. In the places that have been right under the water everything is just mud and rubbish, except at the tops of tall buildings that must have stuck up above it. But now and then—especially at the start of the voyage when we were up in hilly country—you find bits of high ground that the water never covered, and then the buildings are in a better state, fairly tumbledown, but full of tables and chairs and pictures and books and pots and pans and what-have-you.

We often wonder about them, the People. Specially Stanley. I suppose you could say he's got a bit of an obsession with them. He's studying them, he says, so that in the end he'll be an expert on them. Stanley's great on being an expert at things; at one time or another he's claimed to be an expert on just about everything.

We wonder where the People went. Stanley thinks they went to the stars. He sits sometimes at night and gawps at the stars and the moon and gets very intense and mystical and says things like There's Someone Up There. It makes Freda very irritated. "How can there be?" she says. "They'd fall off, wouldn't they? Those things are high up, you can see that. Anyone up there would fall off, like off trees, stands to reason." And Stanley gets impatient and says you've got no imagination, that's your trouble, you only see things as they are, not how they might be, you don't have Ideas, like me. Freda just sniffs and says good thing one of us has got some common sense, that's all I can say.

But there's no getting away from it, if it hadn't been for some of Stanley's ideas, we'd never have finished the voyage. (But then of course if it wasn't for Stanley we'd never have made it in the first place.) Take the boat, for

5

instance: that was Stanley's idea, whatever Ned may claim.

The boat is called QV 66 PROPERTY OF THE PORT OF LONDON AUTHORITY RETURN TO DEPOT 3. It is wide and flat and big and strong enough for both Ned and Freda to get on to it, though then the water tends to come in through the hole at one end, and either Stanley has to plug it up with things or Freda has to sit on it, which she doesn't like because she says it gives her rheumatism. In the beginning, when we started, we could only drift with the current, and it didn't seem as though really the boat would be much use because you couldn't keep it going in any particular direction, and then Stanley had one of his brilliant ideas that he gets if only he can concentrate long enough, and he fixed up a sort of plank at the back, with strings that he could pull, and after that he could steer QV 66 and make it go pretty well the way he wanted.

Stanley found it just outside Carlisle, soon after we began the voyage. It was drifting around at the edge of the water and Stanley stood staring at it for a bit, and then suddenly he said, "*I* know . . . *I* know how we'll get to London. I've just had one of my brilliant ideas, in fact it's probably the most brilliant idea I've ever had . . ."

But I'm getting ahead of the story. I'd better go back.

Back to how we came to be with Stanley in the first place.

Freda and I found him under a bush. I'd gone into this bush after a rabbit and instead of a rabbit there was Stanley. I came shooting out backwards and said to Freda, "There's a horrible thing in there. A horrible creature like nothing I ever saw before."

Freda said, "Better leave it alone then—be on the safe side." But she's curious, too, so we both poked our noses into the bush again and poor Stanley came creeping out, very dirty and bedraggled and shaking all over because he thought I was going to eat him. When I want to annoy him I say there was never any danger of that because I don't eat trash. The fact is we were both fascinated, Freda and I. We stared and stared at him and Freda said, "I think there's something wrong with it. I think it was meant to be something else but it went wrong when it was very young."

And Stanley burst into tears and said, "I'm not an It. I'm a Who."

Stanley is very free with his emotions. He has a lot of them and he doesn't do much about controlling them. At least that's one way of putting it. What he says is that he's got feelings and what's the point of having feelings if you don't enjoy them? Personally I think you should be a bit more moderate, but that's just my opinion.

The fact is, Stanley has problems—or he had them. It's no fun, he used to say, being the only one of you. It's all very well for you lot—you see other cows and horses and dogs or whatever all over the place. You don't know what it's like to be stared at all the time and have people making comments about you. I'm sure, he used to say pathetically, I must have got some friends and relations somewhere. It's not that I want to stop with them necessarily. I just want to see them, have a look at them, find out what I am. Nobody wants to spend the rest of their life thinking they're some kind of mistake. I just want to know there's someone else like me, somewhere.

Which is how it came about that the voyage of QV 66 began. . . . But I'm getting ahead again.

As I say, Freda and I found Stanley under this bush, and immediately after that he almost got done for by some dogs. They were out rabbiting, too, like me, only they were in a pack (I've never been much of a one for packs, myself, I'd rather operate on my own) and they caught sight of Stanley and at once they all started bawling to each other, "Get after it! Kill it!" Stanley dived back into the bush again but they surrounded it and a nasty-looking terrier was all set to go in after him. I said, "Leave it alone, can't you—it's not a rabbit." They said they could see that all right but they were going to have it anyway, just for fun. "It's got no right being here," they said, "a queer-looking thing like that."

And then Freda started getting all truculent. She put her head down and poked her horns at them and said, "Why not, then?" Freda can be very unpredictable at times; you never quite know how she'll take things. And she's soft-hearted and she doesn't like unpleasantness. She'll get quite unpleasant herself putting a stop to it.

The terrier said, "It's different, that's why. You can't have animals going round being different. Come on, boys."

And that did it, as far as we were concerned. Freda gave a great bellow and charged at them. She had them dashing in all directions to get out of her way until eventually they cleared off, while I saw to the terrier personally; I just don't happen to care for that type. And when they'd gone Stanley eventually crawled out of the bush and rolled up in a small hairy ball with just his tail curling out and moaned, "Please don't be nasty to me. I'm harmless and unimportant, in fact I'm not really here at all." We said we had no intention of being nasty to him, and presently he unrolled himself and his small wrinkled face with its shiny black eyes peered thoughtfully at us and after a while he perked up and became considerably less humble and more like the Stanley we were—had we but known it— fated to know so well.

And that was it, somehow. We came together, the six of us, and we stayed together. I can't remember, now, why Freda and I were together in the first place, when we found Stanley. Freda says she'd adopted me, which of

8

course is ridiculous. I think we'd just met casually. Ned says he turned up at about the same time and helped get rid of the dogs, and Offa says he was on his way from Durham Cathedral to York Minster (he got blown off the front of Lichfield in a gale and has been trying to find it again ever since) and came down to see what all the fuss was about.

So you see that was about the sum of it: we started off feeling sorry for Stanley, and a bit protective, and then we got more and more intrigued by him. He gets you, does Stanley. Mind, he can be exasperating—but just when he's at his most maddening and you decide you've had about enough of him he'll do a sudden switch and be quite different. I sometimes think he's about six different animals, is Stanley. He's never boring, I'll say that. He tells stories better than any of us. We all tell stories but ours are mostly about what's happened to us, or what we think has happened to us. Stanley's are weird. He tells stories about how when the sun goes down at night it turns into a golden fish and swims about, and that's why you must never go into the water at night or you might make it angry and it won't come up again in the morning. He tells stories about how the stars sing and how you can catch the wind if you run fast enough, and he says there are animals who live in the clouds. Look, he says, you can see the shapes of them. Freda says, "That's not true, Stanley. You're making that up, aren't you?" And Stanley looks at her and says, "I don't know. P'raps I am and p'raps I'm not."

Freda says sternly, "It's not nice to say things that aren't true." But after he first told the golden fish story she went down to the water and stared into it for a long time one night. She said she was just having a drink, but I'm not so sure about that.

I suppose you could say that in a funny way Stanley is

9

our leader, if anyone is. Not that he's good at leading (he gets into a panic at crucial moments, as you will hear) but just that he seems to be important.

And that is how we set out, how and why. To find out what Stanley is. After he found the picture.

The picture was in Carlisle Station. We'd fetched up there, the six of us, one day not so long after we came together. Stanley loved stations. He liked bustling around the trains, investigating everything and fiddling with the machinery and helping himself to anything he fancied. Ned and Freda were wandering about the platforms complaining that there wasn't any grass and Offa was swooping around the roof and saying that it wasn't a patch on a first-class cathedral. Stanley had been climbing on to one of the engines trying to puzzle out how it worked. He says the People went around in trains, hundreds of them at a time, but he can't for the life of him see how they made them go. Same with cars—there are the rusty hulks of them all over the place and Stanley pulls them to bits and pores over them but he can't see how they worked. It makes him very cross.

Anyway, he had got bored with the engine and was playing about with some machines he'd found that still had rolls and rolls of paper ribbon in them. He was pulling this out and wrapping it round himself and capering around doing a kind of dance to attract our attention. None of us were watching; Stanley is a terrible show-off and we'd learned by then to take no notice. "Very funny, young Stanley," grunted Ned. "Very humorous. And now let's push off somewhere where there's grass, shall we?" And then all of a sudden Stanley stopped prancing about and let out a great gasp. He'd seen the picture.

It was a picture of someone like him. Sitting on the branch of a tree looking out at us. And underneath was

10

printed in large black letters VISIT LONDON ZOO. SPECIAL WEEKEND EXCURSION RATE £10 CHILDREN HALF-PRICE.

"Well, I never," said Freda. "There you are, Stanley, you're not a mistake after all."

Stanley was overcome for a while. He just sat and stared at the picture. And then he went mad. He did cartwheels over the luggage trolleys and climbed right up to the top of the station and swung from the roof and hung by his tail from a notice that said Buffet and Bar. He was quite out of control. Then he came leaping down and said to us, "Let's go and find them. Now. Today."

"Steady on, old son," said Ned. "We don't know where it is."

"Yes, we do," said Stanley. "London, it says. London Zoo. Oh, please," he went on plaintively, "can't we go there and see my friends and relations and find out what I am?"

We looked at each other. Pansy said what fun, are we going to have an adventure, and then went off to chase a butterfly she had noticed. Pansy is rather irresponsible; that is partly because she is young but I suspect it is also her character. Freda, who was feeling sorry for Stanley and didn't want him to be disappointed, said well we can always try dear, but better not be too upset if nothing comes of it.

I said, "I wonder where London is?"

We knew that the People gave names to all their places —from big town down to the smallest village—because the names are still there, on the road signs. The signs have numbers on them, too, and we'd wondered from time to time what the numbers meant, but it didn't seem to matter much so we didn't go on bothering about it. Offa, who was perched on top of the picture, looking pensive, said suddenly, "London 307. Just thought I'd mention it. Hosanna! I shall lift up mine eyes unto the hills! Road sign outside the station—noticed it just now."

As I have said, Offa is a somewhat eccentric bird, owing to the unusual circumstances of his youth.

"Three hundred and seven whats?" said Pansy idly, having lost the butterfly and returned to the conversation.

Stanley gave a kind of squeak. "Stop!" he said. He put his head in his hands. "Wait," he moaned. "I've got it! No, I haven't . . . Don't anybody talk, I'm having a headache about it."

Stanley's headaches usually lead to one of his ideas. He sits there moaning and groaning and complaining and eventually bounces around in triumph with one of his brilliant ideas. At least sometimes. Sometimes he just has a headache and nothing happens.

This time, though, after about three minutes during which we all watched him anxiously (except Pansy who had found another butterfly), he sat up and said breathlessly, "It's how far away places are. Big numbers like two hundred mean they are a long way away and little ones like three mean they are quite near."

"Fancy that," said Freda. "That's ever so clever of you, Stanley, I must say."

"I know," said Stanley modestly. "What you do is, you shut your eyes and kind of squeeze up the inside of your head so all the thoughts are very loud and clear and then you have to try and fix on the one you're interested in and your headache gets worse and worse and . . ."

I said, "Three hundred and seven means a very long way indeed."

There was a silence. Stanley began to droop. His tail, which had been a tight and sprightly spiral, sagged and uncoiled. "All right," he said mournfully. "It doesn't matter. Never mind. I don't really *care*. Just it would be nice to *see* if I'm the only one like me in the world or not . . . Just one would like to *know*, that's all." His black eyes glistened. "Oh, it doesn't really *matter*," he went on. "I daresay we wouldn't ever have got there anyway."

There was a further silence, shorter. "Right you are, then, mate," said Ned. "I suppose a bit of exercise'll do us no harm. Better get started then, eh?"

So that, you see, is how the voyage of QV 66 began.

2

In which QV 66 is hijacked, a box of matches comes in handy, Stanley has one of his brilliant ideas and the animals take to the road

I told you earlier how, soon after that, we found the boat. It was just as well, or we would probably have abandoned the whole idea of the voyage, there and then, once it dawned on us precisely what we were trying to do. In the first place, there was water in all directions: in the second, we only had the vaguest idea which direction to take. Offa, who does a good deal of flying around to explore and prospect, followed up Stanley's brilliant idea about what the numbers on the People's road signs meant by working out that they stood for distances called miles (he spotted a different kind of sign somewhere). The rest of us, he said, couldn't walk more than about ten miles in a day, which made three hundred and seven of them seem very daunting. But, more important, there was water on every side.

We thought we could keep going in the general direction of London by following the road signs, or even the roads themselves. The roads were sometimes very overgrown and grassy but they were always easy enough to see— especially the big wide ones—and plenty of them had signs that spoke of London. Offa could always fly on ahead to investigate, too. But the trouble was that there was so much water around. Wherever there was a river or stream valley It had become a lake, and the roads would vanish into these great stretches of water, so that to keep going in the right direction you had to find some way of crossing the water. And that, until Stanley spotted QV 66 and had his next brilliant idea, seemed quite impossible.

The boat changed everything. With it, we were no longer restricted to the dry ground. We could take to the water. In fact, it was very much easier and quicker to travel by water. The problem, of course, was that in order to have QV 66 for the water, we had to take it with us on land.

"What!" said Ned, when the suggestion was first put to him. "You must be joking, mate!"

"It's perfectly easy," said Stanley, bustling around with a length of rope he had scavenged from somewhere. "Just stand still a minute, could you. . . . Actually it's not really my idea because I've seen a picture of the People doing it with animals like you, but all the same it's rather clever of me to have thought of it. . . ."

Ned made a considerable fuss, and I must admit one can't blame him. The boat was heavy, and although it was flat-bottomed and slid fairly well over grass or smooth places, it was very hard work for him to pull it up hills or when the going was rough. Even Stanley could appreciate this. He kept scowling and frowning, staring at the boat and Ned and the rope which joined them together. "There's something not quite right," he muttered. "Something's got left out but I can't think what it is."

The boat had become not only our transport but a kind of home as well. Stanley would sit up at the back, steering, with his box beside him. The box had all his precious things in it—bits of junk he'd collected from here and there and insisted on keeping in case they came in useful. It's a big wooden box called GRADE 1 APPLES HANDLE WITH CARE that he found and it's crammed full of his belongings. Stanley used to play with them for hours; at least he said it was working, not playing. He said he was finding out what they were for. He had a lot of metal tools he'd picked up in factories; he said he knew the People used them for making things with—they made everything in the world with them, he thought—but he couldn't for the moment see how they did it. One day, he said, he'd have an idea and find out. They had lots of these tools in their houses, too, the People. Stanley had various things he'd picked up in ruined houses: a collection of little glass balls with different coloured threads twisting around inside them, that he sometimes let Pansy play with, and a bright orange stick with a little brush at one end that he grooms himself with and another stick that makes a noise if he blows into it. He says those are not serious things, but he spends quite a lot of time working with them, I've noticed. He'd got lots of tools, and some books, too.

We quite often find books; sometimes we've found whole ruins with nothing else in them so we know the People thought they were important, since they made houses specially for them. Stanley says it's a pity there isn't time to read them all, because some of them tell stories and there are lots he'd like to keep. He'd only got three, though, then, and a pile of newspapers that he used to cover himself up with at night when it was cold (Stanley feels the cold a lot, which he says is another thing that proves he has stronger feelings than the rest of us; personally I think it's because he has less fur). The newspapers all said at the top *The Times* and underneath, in smaller print, things like PRIME MINISTER ASSURES NATION

16

NO CALL FOR ALARM ON FLOOD WARNINGS, and POPE PRAYS FOR DIVINE INTERVENTION, and AMERICA AND RUSSIA TO ORGANISE WORLD EVACUATION TO MARS. In fact they have writing all over them but it's all very boring so we've never bothered to read them properly.

One of the books is nearly all pictures. Stanley loves it. He says it tells a story in pictures and he's always looking at it. It's called *Asterix*. The other book is called the *Shorter Oxford English Dictionary* and Stanley only kept it because it was the biggest book he ever found so he says presumably it's the best. It made a good seat for when he was steering the boat. He said it wasn't very good for reading because it didn't tell a story but it had a great many long words in it that he used to study from time to time. He said most of them you wouldn't really need very often, perhaps only once in your life, but it was nice to know they were there in case you wanted them.

It was only a few days after we had found the boat and started the voyage that Stanley came across a whole lot of things in a house that had not been under the water and was going through them to see if they were more precious than the things he'd got already, or not, in which case he'd throw them away. One of them was a box full of little sticks with knobby pink ends. A torn label on it had a picture of a swan and said Matches. Stanley thought it must be some kind of game. He spread them all out and made patterns with them and then he got bored with that and started messing about trying to draw a picture with one of them. He loves drawing—his most precious things of all are some coloured sticks for drawing with. He started trying to draw on the box and then suddenly there was the most tremendous squeal and there was Stanley jumping up and down howling and sucking his fingers.

"It bit me!" he said.

We all came over and had a look. "Don't be silly, dear," said Freda. "Sticks don't bite."

"These do," said Stanley. He picked up the match, gingerly, and looked at it. The pink end had gone black now, and it had a funny smell. Stanley touched it with one finger, and yelped again. "Hot!" he said.

"Best let that alone," said Ned.

But Stanley can never let things alone. He picked up another of the matches, and scraped it on the little box, and suddenly it spurted fire, a little tiny fire, not like the big fires we've seen sometimes in forests or rubbish places, and kept well away from. Stanley dropped it quickly and the little fire went out.

"Well, I never!" said Freda. "I don't think you ought to play with those things, Stanley. That could hurt you, that could."

But Stanley was entranced. Not all the matches would

make fires, in fact not many of them would. But he made two or three of them do it, and then he found that if he gave the matches leaves and things to eat the fires would get bigger. Freda didn't like that. She fussed around telling him to stop it. He made himself a little fire and sat crooning at it and warming his hands until it began to rain and the fire got sadder and smaller and went out. He only had a few matches left now.

I said, "Why don't you keep the rest of them for another time?" and Stanley nodded solemnly and said that was a good idea. He put the rest of the matches back in their little box and put the box with the rest of his precious things. He said they were the most precious thing of all now, and given what happened next I must say he was perfectly right.

We'd been moving for quite a long time and Freda was complaining that she hadn't had a good graze all day, so we tied the boat up and everybody wandered off. Ned and Freda were eating, Pansy was asleep in the sun and Stanley was squatting under a tree, fiddling with one of his tools. His box of matches was beside him. Offa had found a nice patch of brussels sprouts, and I was busy giving some rabbits a bit of exercise. And then all of a sudden we heard Stanley making that shrill chattering noise he produces when something's got him in a state. He was pointing at the river.

The boat was no longer where we had left it.

I said, "Offa, go and see if you can spot it."

Offa went flapping off and after a few minutes he came back and said, "It's downstream, not very far."

"That's all right, then," I said. "The rope must've come untied. We'll go and find it."

Offa said, "No, it didn't come untied. Somebody took it."

"Who?" said Ned, snorting.

"Some dogs. A pack. They look nasty."

"Soon sort them out," I said, and I set off down the river bank with everybody else behind me, Freda saying, "Now don't let's have any unpleasantness, I'm sure it's all some kind of mistake, you wouldn't get anyone taking something that belonged to someone else on *purpose*, now, would you?"

You were beginning to get animals ganging up together, in those days, and it's a funny thing, but they always seem to behave worse like that than in the normal way of things. Like those dogs that tried to kill Stanley. And this lot. These were a bunch of proper riff-raff and there they were scurrying about all over our boat, behaving in a thoroughly vulgar way. They'd got Stanley's box open and one of them was chewing the *Shorter Oxford English Dictionary*. Stanley howled with fury.

I said, "That's our boat, if you don't mind. Would you please get out of it?"

"Why?" shouted one of them.

"Because it's ours," I said patiently. "We're going somewhere in it."

"Then you'll have to go somewhere out of it, won't you?" he shouted, and of course they all thought that was hilarious.

"Well!" said Freda indignantly. "I must say! I don't think that's right at all. They've got no business."

And then they spotted Stanley. "Cor!" they said. "What's that? Something the cat brought in! I say, mate, you want to take a look at yourself! Someone slipped up there all right! Funnyface! Bighead!"

"You get out of that boat!" bawled Ned, stamping up and down. Even Pansy was spitting and hissing. Freda was mooing on about how it wasn't nice to talk about other people like that.

I barked, "You just get out of that boat, or you'll be sorry!"

"Make us!" they said, laughing their heads off.

Stanley was in a frenzy. I knew what he was thinking. Boats aren't two a penny. We've come across others, from time to time, but usually all leaky or the wrong shape. Never a flat one like this, that we can all get on to. No QV 66, he was thinking, no London. "Get out of it!" he shrieked at those dogs, and they just yipped with laughter all the more and QV 66 drifted away from us down the river. "Funnyface!" they shouted. "Four-eyes! Who d'you think you are, anyway!"

"I'll tell you what he is," bellowed Ned. "He's a lot cleverer than you scum, any day."

"Prove it!" yelped the dogs.

"All right," screamed Stanley. "I will! Watch this!" And he took one of the matches out of the box and rubbed it on the side and by one of those bits of good luck that Stanley has sometimes it worked. It spouted fire and Stanley grabbed hold of a dry branch and set light to that and waved it around. "There!" he said. "Let's see you do that."

The dogs all crowded to the edge of QV 66 and gawped at him. One or two of them were whining. Nobody likes fire. In fact everybody's dead scared of it. You don't know where it comes from or where it goes to or what makes it. You run away from it, quick. The dogs shifted around nervously. And just then I noticed that QV 66 was drifting towards the bank; in a minute or two she was going to be nicely stuck against an overhanging tree. I said something to Stanley. His branch was burning away now and dropping sparks around.

"Get out of that boat!" I bawled at the dogs. "Get out of it sharpish—or he throws the fire at you."

QV 66 ground against the bank, rocked around a bit, and came to a halt against the tree. "Right!" I said to Stanley, and Stanley went rushing towards it, making dreadful howling noises and waving the branch around.

"Oh dear, oh dear!" moaned Freda. "Now we don't want anyone to get hurt, do we? Why can't everybody just be sensible?"

The dogs barked and rushed about and then they jumped for the bank, knocking into each other in their hurry to be off, pushing and shoving so that several of them fell into the river and had to scramble out farther down, weeping and wailing. "That'll teach you!" I bawled after them. "You thieving lot of rubbish! Clear out. He can fly, too!" That sent them off with their tails between their legs, I can tell you.

Stanley was yelping now, because sparks from the branch were singeing his fur and he'd burned one of his hands. He hurled the branch into the river where it lay sizzling in the water for a minute or two, and then he jumped on to QV 66 and did a victory dance, sucking his sore hand at the same time.

Well, we'd learned a lesson. Several lessons. One was not to leave the boat unguarded, and another was that there are some nasty people around. Freda couldn't get over it. She went on and on about how you'd never have got that kind of behaviour when she was young and she didn't know what things were coming to. Pansy sat purring at Stanley and opening and closing her eyes at him and saying, "I think you're wonderful, Stanley."

"I know I am," said Stanley.

"Now, Stanley," said Freda. "That's not a nice way to talk, is it?" But Stanley's the type that's up one minute and down the next, and we all thought that after that he was entitled to a bit of up, so we had a long storytelling session that night, sitting snug on QV 66, and Stanley told a story he'd just thought of about a creature who sounded suspiciously like him who was always getting the better of people bigger and stronger than him because of his clever tricks and ideas. "Now that's going too far," Freda would say. "Now, Stanley, you don't expect us to believe that, do you?", but I noticed she went on listening all the same.

We were getting into a very mountainous place. The land got steeper and steeper and there were fewer big stretches of water, and what there was wound around between the hills so that sometimes we'd find ourselves going almost in a circle and ending on the other side of the same hill. And there weren't many roads—that was the worst of it. And the ones that there were had no more signs to London. We drifted about from one small place to another, and it rained and rained and rained, and we all got rather bad-tempered. Ned met up with some other horses and started muttering about how he might just stop here and he wasn't a great one for travel anyway and one place was much the same as another, wasn't it? But when it came to the point and we moved on he stopped all that and came too. He said he seemed to be stuck with the rest of us, now. And anyway, he said, he supposed he'd better hang around and find out what Stanley was.

When we'd ended up twice in a place called Ullswater we decided something had to be done about finding out which way we ought to be going, so we sent Offa to try and find a road with signs to London on it. He was gone for so long that we thought something awful must have happened to him, and then at last after a couple of days he turned up again, very tired and bedraggled. He'd been blown off course, he said, time and again, and he'd had a very unpleasant experience he didn't want to talk about with a falcon, but eventually he'd found a road pointing to London. And he'd been talking to other birds, he said, and they'd told him that if you weren't careful you got to the edge of the world near here, where the water went on for ever and ever. They said it was wild water, without islands or the tops of trees, and there was no end to it anywhere, and the sun goes down into it at night. "I'd like to see that," said Stanley, interested, but Freda shuddered and said you wouldn't know where you were with a place like that. Offa said that the other birds had told him, too, that the mountains ended after a while, if we followed the roads going towards London, and we'd get to more water, so that it would be easier going. There were big rivers, they said, and huge ruined cities as large as hundreds of fields put together, and plenty of roads.

It took us a long time to get out of the mountains, but at last the land began to get flatter. The trouble was that the rivers were getting narrower, too. Sometimes the boat would be stuck fast and we'd have to spend half the day pushing and pulling to get it free, or Ned would have to drag it from one bit of water to another. It got more and more difficult. Freda said she thought we ought to leave it behind and walk, but then Offa pointed out that we were going to get to more water later on, and we'd need it then or we wouldn't be able to get any farther at all, like the flocks of sheep we met from time to time in the hills, trapped on islands by the water. They didn't seem to mind particularly, so long as there was enough grazing, and they obviously thought we were mad to be moving around all the time. They used to stare and stare at Stanley and pass remarks about him out of the sides of their mouths, so that you couldn't quite catch what they said. Stanley didn't particularly care. "Who wants to be them, any-way?" he said. "All exactly alike, so you can't tell t'other from which, just standing there chewing grass all day."

"I thought that was what you wanted, Stanley," said Pansy sweetly. "Someone just like you."

"That's different," said Stanley. "It's to prove something, isn't it?" And he sat in front of the sheep fiddling around with some of the most complicated things out of his box, just to show them how busy and important he was.

"I'll tell you something, young Stanley," said Ned. "It's time you had another one of these bright ideas of yours, instead of fooling around like that. You got the boat back off those dogs—now find out some way of making it go by itself." He was very cross and tired; he'd had to heave QV 66 a long way that day.

Stanley pretended not to hear, but you could see quite well he had. He was a bit put out. He doesn't like anyone making fun of his ideas. As he says, and I suppose he's got a point, he's the only one of us who has them.

It was just after that that he found a new book. He found it in the ruins of a house. It was called *The Handyman's Guide to Do-it-Yourself* and it had pictures of People in it, as well as writing.

"What are they doing?" said Pansy, looking over Stanley's shoulder. "Ugh! Weren't they ugly! What's that one doing, hitting something with a kind of stick?"

"I don't know," said Stanley. "I think it's telling a story. I think it's a story about one of them who was a magician and put spells on things and turned them into different things and one day . . ."

"Look," said Pansy. "There's a thing like you've got in your box—the long thing with little teeth. He's cutting a stick in half with it."

Stanley stared at the picture. His eyes got very big and round and he stared and stared and then he rolled about and moaned and then he got up and jumped up and down

26

and then he sat and looked at the book again. "What's the matter?" said Pansy.

"Can't you *see*?" said Stanley.

"No."

"It's a book that tells you how to *make* things. And I've got some of the things to make them out of in my box."

"Oh," said Pansy, unconcerned. She lives in a world of her own, does Pansy.

Stanley went quite mad then. He rushed back to the boat clutching the book and emptied everything out of his box and then squatted in front of the book matching up his bits of metal with the bits of metal in the pictures. Tools. "These are tools," he said, to anyone who would listen. "This is a hammer and this is a saw and this is a screwdriver and this that I haven't got one of is a wrench and this that I haven't got either is a pair of pliers."

"Very nice, Stanley," said Freda, comfortably chewing the cud. "Very pretty."

"Not *pretty*!" screamed Stanley, in a frenzy. "*Useful! Important!* You *make things* with them!"

"No need to raise your voice, dear," said Freda.

I could see what Stanley was on about. I sat and watched him, without saying much because when Stanley's trying to concentrate it's best not to interrupt. He's very highly-strung and can be easily put off. He rushed round for the next hour or two finding bits of wood and cutting them up with the saw, and banging nails into them with the hammer, and howling with anguish because he kept hitting his fingers instead, but he wouldn't stop for a moment. Then he got tired of that and went back to that house to see what he could find and came back after a bit with two big thin wheels either side of a seat and an arrangement in front to hold on to. We've come across these before; they're called bicycles, Stanley says, and the People used them to go

27

about on. Anyway, he had a lovely time taking this one to bits with his tools until all he had was a pile of metal and wire and two big wheels, but then of course he couldn't put it together again, so he fixed the seat on to the back of the boat (he said it was more comfortable than the *Shorter Oxford English Dictionary*) and threw the rest away. At that point Ned came along, and gave one of the wheels a kick and said, "That's what we need. Save me a lot of trouble. You want to do something about that, young Stanley."

Stanley's jaw dropped. He stared at the wheels and then at the boat and then at Ned, who was wandering off to look for some more grazing, and then he shouted after him, "I'm just going to, aren't I? I can't do everything at once, can I?"

Ned came back and looked at the wheels again. "You could put things like that on the boat?"

"Yes," said Stanley. "I think so," he added, more cautiously.

"That'd be champion," said Ned, impressed. Everybody had crowded round now: even Pansy could see that this might be important. "Can't you put those ones on?" she said.

"No," said Stanley. "They're the wrong shape, somehow. It wouldn't work. You want smaller ones. And thicker."

"Right," I said. "Everybody keeps their eye out, from now on. It's the most important thing, next to food."

It took us days to find any. We were in a part that must have been under the water for a long time and all the rubbish was rusted up and broken and Stanley said he couldn't do anything with it. And then at last Offa came back from some exploratory flying around and said he thought he'd found what Stanley wanted, only they were

28

stuck on to something. So Stanley and I went off with him and sure enough there was a big wooden thing with four wheels, just the right size and with thick hard rubber tyres on them instead of the thin kind that most wheels have, and that are usually broken when we find them.

Stanley had an awful time getting them off the wooden thing they were fixed on to. He fiddled about and banged and heaved and pushed and sometimes he got so worked up he had to stop and rush up and down trees, howling with rage. Offa and I got very frustrated, not being able to help. Offa kept chanting bits of stuff he learned when he was young in Lichfield Cathedral, meaning, I suppose, to keep Stanley's spirits up. He sat there saying, "Oh God our help in ages past our hope for years to come," and things like that which made Stanley very irritated. There wasn't anything I could do so I just made noises of encouragement and admiration every now and then and at last with a final heave Stanley got the last wheel off.

"There!" he said. "Get Ned."

He tied the wheels together with a bit of rope and Ned pulled them back to the boat and then Stanley got the most dreadful headache and crawled under a bush and stayed there by himself for two days, with his *Handyman's Guide to Do-it-Yourself*. We all hunted for things he specially likes, such as apples and nuts and berries, and put them in front of the bush and Stanley's small hairy hand would come out and take them and then retreat inside again, and then at last he emerged and said, "Nails. Screws. Axles. Bolts. Nuts—not the kind you eat."

We said, "What?"

"Oh, you're hopeless, you lot," said Stanley. "No brains. Come on." And he went dashing off back to the place where Offa found the wheels and spent all day scavenging around and then made us bring back a lot of bits and pieces to the boat. Then he got to work again.

After two more days the boat had four wheels.

"Stanley," said Ned solemnly, "you are amazing, and that's a fact."

Offa said, "Hosanna unto the highest. Alleluia!"

"Do shut up," said Stanley. He was in a very excited state, twittering and jumping around. "Ned, get the rope and pull it up there."

We were in a grassy place at the foot of a hill. There were some sheep grazing on the hillside and no one else around. "Up there?" said Ned doubtfully.

"Yes," said Stanley. "Come on."

"Now Stanley," said Freda nervously, "don't you go doing anything rash. We don't want all this to end in tears, do we?"

But there was no stopping him. He made Ned pull the boat up to the top of the slope and then he unhitched the rope and sat on his bicycle seat at the back and said, "Now push!"

"Well!" said Ned. "I don't think really . . ."

"Push!"

So Ned gave the back of the boat a great heave and it went trundling off down the hill, slowly at first, with Stanley sitting there at the back whooping with triumph, and then it got faster and faster until it was fairly hurtling down and Stanley's whoops had changed to shrieks of alarm and finally the boat crashed into some bushes at the bottom and tipped over on to its side, and Stanley came spinning out and ended up head downwards in some brambles.

"There!" said Freda. "What did I say?"

"How are the mighty fallen!" droned Offa. "Tell it not in Gath, publish it not in the streets of Askelon."

We helped Stanley out of the brambles and got the boat

right side up again. Stanley picked the thorns out of himself and looked at us a bit sheepishly and said, "Well, it works, anyway."

3

In which Stanley nearly drowns and is rescued by a very superior bird; we proceed to Manchester, Freda finds a hat, we look at some pictures, and disaster strikes again

We got along a great deal more easily after that. We could take to the land whenever we wanted to and there was no great difficulty for Ned about pulling the boat: it trundled along quite smoothly. We could use the People's roads, too, which made it a simpler matter to keep going in the right direction. Stanley, I'm afraid, was really rather impossible for quite a while, though. He soon forgot about the episode of the bramble-bush, and became extremely conceited and self-important. He also got very lazy and made the rest of us chase around finding him food: he said he was so clever and sensitive that he had to be careful not to wear himself out. "Where would you be without me?" he said. "Stuck, that's what." So we had to remind him that if it wasn't for him we wouldn't be making this voyage anyway. "Set up with a nice bit of grazing somewhere, having a quiet life, that's what I'd be doing," said Ned. "Not pulling that wretched boat from one end of the world to the other." At which Stanley sighed theatrically and said that some people don't know when they're well off. Lot of stick-in-the-muds, that's what you are, he said. Here am I trying to broaden your outlooks, *show* you things, and you talk to me about grazing. Some people, he went on, might be *grateful* to be associating with a genius. Some people might be *glad*.

"Some people might give him a clip round the earhole if he's not careful," grumbled Ned, and I must say at that point the rest of us agreed with him. Stanley can be very trying, as you've no doubt gathered, and he was at his most trying then. In view of which perhaps what happened next was no bad thing. It brought him down to earth again. Except that as it turned out it wasn't exactly earth.

We'd got to a place where suddenly the hills had begun to level out and there was a great big expanse of water ahead. Offa had flown on to prospect and reported that the other side seemed to be a long way away, though there were one or two smallish islands dotted around and the usual things sticking up by way of telegraph poles and the tops of chimneys and here and there a church spire. He reckoned that we didn't at the moment need to cross this bit of water but could keep going down the side of it, using the boat when we needed to negotiate a water channel. Quite often the road we were following would dip down and disappear under a reach of water: now that we had wheels on QV 66 we could just go straight on and out the other side, if we could pick up the road again.

There was a high wind. Wind always has an odd effect on Stanley—it makes him over-excited. He was behaving quite ridiculously that day, fooling about and doing tricks and generally showing off. He sat on Ned's back jigging up and down and saying "Gee-up, gee-up," which gets Ned in a proper temper, and one can hardly blame him, and then when we stopped at the edge of the water to debate which way we were going next, he swarmed up to the top of a high tree and swung from branch to branch, chanting that he was The Greatest.

"Oh, shut up, Stanley," I said.

Stanley came slithering down and said in an aggrieved voice, "You don't like me, do you?"

I said, "Of course I do, Stanley. It's just that you're being a bit annoying. Do be quiet."

"Oh, you're all so *serious*," said Stanley. He did some somersaults and made a few funny faces to show how witty he was, but nobody took any notice so he hunted around for something else to attract attention. He delved in his box and came out with a piece of bright red material he'd found somewhere and wrapped it round himself and strutted about. Freda said, "That colour doesn't really suit you, dear." Stanley unwrapped the material and draped it round the end of the boat like a flag and fidgeted about, looking for something else. Then he picked up a basket that he'd collected a few days before (it had been useful for carrying a whole lot of apples that he'd found) and put it on his head like a hat and peered out through the wickerwork, hopefully. Pansy giggled and said, "You do look funny, Stanley."

Encouraged, Stanley capered around a bit with the basket and then he rushed up the tree again, carrying it with one of his back hands, and hung it from one of the topmost branches. Then he got into it.

The branch hung right out over the water. Ned said, "You want to watch what you're doing, young Stanley."

Pansy said, "Ooh, Stanley, are you going to fall in?"

"'Course not," said Stanley. He stood up in his basket and jigged around. "Look at me! Yoo-hoo, Freda. Look at me!"

There was a splintering noise. The end of the branch broke off and came splashing down into the water, and with it the basket. And in the basket, Stanley.

The basket landed in the water with a splash and for a moment we lost sight of it. And then it bobbed up on the far side of the tree, with Stanley's horrified face peering out over the edge. He was clinging on for dear life, both hands holding the edge and his tail curled round the handle. We heard him say "Help!" faintly.

As I've said, there was a high wind. The water was choppy, flecked with little white waves, and flowing fast. The basket began at once to drift quickly away from the shore. Even as we watched it moved away five yards, ten, fifteen. . . . At first we were too shocked to do anything, and then we all rushed up and down at the edge, telling each other what to do. "Get the boat out!" Freda wailed. "Go and fetch him with the boat. Quick!"

But we'd decided, just a few minutes before, when Stanley was fooling about, that it was too rough to take the boat on the water. I hesitated a moment, and saw that it would be madness to put the boat out, especially without Stanley to steer it. We couldn't possibly control it and the chances of it reaching Stanley were almost non-existent. Freda saw that too, as soon as she had spoken. We looked at each other in consternation.

"Not to worry, Stanley old son," bellowed Ned. "We'll get you out of it. Just you keep your head, that's all."

"Help! Oh, please help!" came from Stanley. Faintly now, as the basket drifted farther and farther away, sometimes bobbing out of sight behind the waves.

"Stanley, you hold on tight!" called Freda. "Just be sensible and try not to get your feet wet."

We were worried, I can tell you. I couldn't for the life of me think what to do. Of course, there was always the chance that the wind might change direction and wash the basket up somewhere farther away, possibly on to one of the islands that we could see out in the water. But if that happened the chances of Stanley getting back to us again were pretty remote.

"Oh, poor Stanley," said Pansy, with tears in her eyes,

and at that moment I must say the irritating side of him didn't seem very important. We thought of his good points.

Offa said, "I'll fly out to him. Cheer him up a bit. Alleluia. Hosanna."

And then I had an idea. "Hang on," I said. I hunted around in Stanley's box and found what I'd hoped would be there—a longish piece of string. "Look," I said to Offa, "if you flew out with that in your beak, and dangled it down to him, he could tie it on to the handle . . ."

". . . and I could pull the basket back. Good thinking," said Offa.

We watched anxiously as Offa set off with the string hanging down behind him. The wind was almost a gale now and he was being buffeted about by it, blown from one side to the other and up and down so that it seemed ages before he got to Stanley, who was rapidly becoming just a distant dot on the heaving water. We saw him circling round, and Stanley reaching out, and then we saw him fly up again, and flap around wildly. Freda said, "Oh dear, I don't think he's strong enough, you know."

We could see Offa flapping and tugging and the basket jumping up and down in the water. For what seemed ages we watched, and then we saw Offa drop the string and come flying back, blown hither and thither on the way.

"It's no good," he said breathlessly, "I can't get it to go the way I want, what with the wind and the water. It just pulls me, instead of me pulling it." He looked very doleful and added, "Oh, hear us when we cry to Thee, for those in peril on the sea . . ."

Pansy said suddenly, "Look, the basket's got washed up against something."

We all peered out on to the water. I said, "What is it?" I'm better at smelling than seeing.

Offa said, "It's the top of a church spire. Stanley's

getting out of the basket. There's a weathercock. He's climbed up it and he's sitting on it."

I could just make it out now, as the sun came out for a moment and a shaft of light came down and picked out the bright shining weathercock with Stanley crouched on its back clinging on to its neck for dear life. And then I saw something else in the sky just above, something large and brown, cruising round and round in circles, coming lower all the time.

"Deliver us from evil!" squawked Offa. "The hosts of Satan are upon us! Excuse me a moment." And he dived into the cover of a tree.

"It's some kind of enormous brown bird," said Freda, staring. "Well, I never! I haven't seen one of those before."

The bird circled lazily round and round Stanley and the weathercock for a minute or two. Then, apparently, it caught sight of us on the shore, for it suddenly changed direction and came floating towards us, hardly moving its wings, with just a lazy flap now and then. Offa, in the tree, moaned faintly.

The bird perched on top of a dead tree stump a few yards away and eyed us. It was enormous, about six times the size of Offa, with a great curved beak. We all felt a bit apprehensive, I can tell you. Pansy had scuttled under a bush.

"'Morning," said Ned. "Bit breezy."

The bird said, "Is it edible? That creature out there."

I said firmly, "No."

"What is it?"

"We don't know. We're making a journey to try to find out. As far as we know he's the only one in the world."

"Is that so?" said the bird with interest. "Comes from a distinguished family, does he? Like me. There are

37

eighteen breeding pairs of us, but we're on the increase, I'm glad to say. I'm the Westmorland branch," it added.

"Pleased to meet you," said Ned.

"And there are my cousins up north, the Eagles of the Glen, and over in Wales there's the Eagles of Snowdonia and down in Devon there's a cadet branch of the family on Exmoor. What's your friend's name? And why's he sitting on that thing out there?"

We explained. The eagle gazed reflectively out towards Stanley. In the tree, Offa flapped suddenly and made a noise of alarm. The eagle shot a look at the tree and said, "It's all right, you can come out—I'm not hungry." Offa emerged and flew down to a bush some way away where he sat eyeing the eagle nervously. Pansy came out too and stared at it.

The eagle said, "Given that he seems to be a person of some distinction, I don't mind lending a hand, as you might say. I'll fly him back to you, if you like."

We said we'd really appreciate that.

"Here, you," said the eagle, to Offa. "You'd better come along, and explain to him what the plan is. People tend to find me off-putting, for some reason."

Offa said, "Yes, sir. Of course, sir."

The eagle sailed away again over the water, with Offa flapping desperately behind. We saw them reach the weathercock, and the eagle cruised around while Offa dropped down and perched alongside Stanley for several minutes. Clearly, he was having a job persuading Stanley to have anything to do with the eagle. But at last he flew up, and the eagle floated down and sat on the weathercock's head, and we saw Stanley creep on to his back, and then the eagle took off. A minute later it alighted beside us and Stanley tumbled to the ground and lay there quivering all over, with his eyes shut.

38

I said to the eagle, "Thank you very much. That was extremely kind."

The eagle inclined its head graciously. "One has certain obligations," it said, "in one's position. One's station in life."

"There, now, Stanley," said Freda. "You're all right now, dear."

Stanley groaned feebly and twitched one leg. "I'm dead."

"No, you're not," I said. "Get up now and say thank you."

Stanley opened one eye and saw the eagle and rolled

up into a ball. "Please don't eat me," he squeaked. "I'm nothing. I'm horrible. I'm so unimportant I'm not really here at all. I'm rubbish. I'm a mistake."

The eagle said, "He doesn't seem very distinguished to me. Who's your father?"

Stanley just lay there shivering. I said to him crossly, "There's no need for that, Stanley, you've been enough trouble today already. Nobody's going to hurt you."

Stanley unrolled himself cautiously and gawped at the eagle, who looked superciliously back. "Extraordinary," it said. "Quite extraordinary. I never saw a creature like that before. I don't think they've got much future, frankly."

It stayed with us for the rest of that day. We had the impression, actually, that it was quite glad of a chat. "One has no objection," it said loftily, "to mixing a bit from time to time. Seeing how the other half lives." It was on its way, it explained, to visit its relations down on Exmoor—"One spends the summer down there," it said. "And then up to Scotland of course in August. Do you know Scotland at all?" We said we didn't and the eagle said patronisingly, "No, I daresay not." It wasn't an entirely disagreeable bird, though, and once you got used to those glaring yellow eyes you had to admit that it was rather handsome. Stanley, who was still extremely subdued, sat hunched up at the foot of the tree staring at it and agreeing with everything it said. Presently he recovered himself enough to jump around a bit and turn a few somersaults. The eagle was quite impressed. "Amusing little thing, isn't he?" it said. "Where did you say you were taking him?"

We explained again. The eagle shook its head. "London? Never heard of it. I don't think it can be much of a place. Not in the same class as Snowdon. Ever been to Snowdon?"

We said we hadn't.

40

"Little mountain we've got in Wales," explained the eagle. "Quite pretty. Where did you say this London was?"

I explained that we didn't really know, but had a rough idea in which direction it was and that it was a long way. "About three hundred miles or so."

"What's miles?" asked the eagle.

We explained about them, too. The eagle was very contemptuous. "Of course personally one doesn't have to bother about that kind of thing," it said. "One just cruises until one gets there. But I can see it's more of a problem for you people. Well, I hope you find it. I'll keep a look out myself and let you know if I come across it. One fetches up in some odd places from time to time."

Offa plucked up enough courage to ask it if it had ever come across Lichfield Cathedral. The eagle looked down its beak at him and said naturally one had had a look round a few cathedrals in one's time but one couldn't recall that one in particular. "We prefer castles," it said. "We've got some nice castle roosts in Wales. Harlech. Caernarvon. Nice little places. If you're ever that way I'll show you round."

Eventually, as dusk fell, the eagle left us. He lifted off the tree stump with one great idle flap of his wings and sailed away over the water, getting higher and higher, until he became a minute speck in the sky and then disappeared altogether.

Pansy said, "Phew! Wasn't it *frightening*!"

"Altogether a bit too uppish, if you ask me," said Freda. "Rather full of itself. Are you all right now, Stanley?"

Stanley was feeling pretty humble. He grovelled around saying how foolish he was, and how stupid, and how irritating, and that he couldn't think why we put up with him. "I'm *stupid*," he said. "Stupid and I show off and

I'm a nuisance and now I feel horrible. I could drown myself," he said dramatically. "I'm just not worth while."

"Well, don't do that," said Ned crossly. "We've had quite enough trouble stopping you being drowned."

"I'm a nothing," said Stanley.

"No, you're not," said Pansy comfortingly. "You're quite nice sometimes."

Stanley went away and sat by the edge of the water until it got quite dark, looking sorry for himself. Later on, though, he came back and settled down for the night with the rest of us. Pansy made the mistake of asking him what it had been like on the eagle's back.

There was a pause. "Piece of cake," said Stanley. "As a matter of fact, flying's easy. Simple. People make an awful fuss about it but personally I thought there was nothing to it. As a matter of fact I . . ."

"Stanley," said Ned, "just belt up, will you."

I think Stanley did learn a lesson from that episode. He was quite quiet and sensible for a good while after that. We were travelling through a hilly part, with water around still but a lot of land as well, so that sometimes we'd be taking the boat along roads and other times sailing down rivers or wide valleys. There were a lot of the People's ruined towns. They were becoming larger and larger and blacker and blacker, with many factories and row upon row of houses all the same, thousands and thousands of them. It became obvious to us that the level of the water was getting lower. We kept coming across buildings where there'd be a line to show that the water had once come up to a certain point on them, or places that were quite dry now would be all in a mess of mud and rubbish as though they'd been under water once. We had noticed this before, but thought it was something to do with how much rain there had been. Now, there seemed no doubt that the whole level of the water had sunk.

Freda said anxiously, "P'raps the world's leaking."

"Have I ever told you how the world began?" said Stanley. "It's interesting. You see in the beginning there was just a great ball of fire, like the sun . . ." ("The sun isn't a ball," Pansy broke in. "It's a flat thing, you can see that.") "Be quiet, I'm telling a story . . . Like the sun, and it spun round so fast that a bit flew off it and it got colder and colder and as it got cold it went hard and in the end trees grew and animals like me came . . ."

"Where from?" said Pansy.

"Stanley," said Freda sternly, before he could go on. "You don't know anything more about it than we do, do you?"

"No," said Stanley. "But it's fun guessing, isn't it?"

Myself, I can't follow Stanley when he gets started off on this kind of caper. As far as I'm concerned, things just are, and the hows and the whys are a bit beyond me. But I must admit I like Stanley's stories.

"If you ask me," said Ned, "however it happened someone made a proper mess of it. There's plenty of things that should have been left out—rain and snow and thistles and horseflies to name one or two. I could have made a better job of it myself."

All of a sudden Freda said, "That's nice. Really pretty. You couldn't have made that, Ned."

It had been raining and now there was a great arch of light across the sky, soft stripes of colour merging into one another, very bright against the grey clouds. Stanley said with interest, "I haven't seen one of those before." He stared at it for a moment and then went on, "Nobody *made* it, anyway, that's obvious. It's just there, like us."

43

Freda said dreamily, "Oh, I don't know—I just meant *we* couldn't have. But take complicated things like those." She nodded vaguely towards a clump of buttercups she was about to eat. "I mean, somebody or something must have thought of them. Like the People made those tools of yours, Stanley."

For some reason Stanley found this very irritating. He jumped about disagreeing (Stanley can never disagree sitting still) and then suddenly he went all quiet and sat looking at the sun, which had now come out, shining on the wet leaves. "Look," he said, pointing at them.

"Yes, dear," said Freda. "Someone's made the water go all coloured. Very pretty."

"Not *someone*," shrieked Stanley. "The rain and the sun."

"Don't hold with rain, personally," said Ned. "Like I was saying just now. Should never have been thought of." Stanley flounced off in disgust.

We were in a particularly disagreeable place—the outskirts of some large town crammed full of factories and dirty tumbledown buildings. We kept finding ourselves in that kind of area; it was all very different from the green and hilly parts that we had left behind. We had been travelling for quite a while by then—we are none of us much good at noticing how much time has gone by so I can't be sure how long—and were encouraged by the fact that London did seem to be getting nearer rather than farther. According to the road signs, that is.

But it was confusing, because lots of the roads said London, so that you'd follow one for a bit and then find it joined up with another one that seemed to be going in a different direction. Offa flew on ahead and reported that we were on the edges of an enormous place – so big you couldn't see from one side of it to the other, just miles and miles of streets and houses. It was called Manchester. There were huge buildings in the middle, he said, bigger than we'd ever seen. Stanley was interested; he wanted to go and have a look. Freda wasn't keen—she doesn't like towns—but in the end he persuaded her. "Don't you want to go and see, Freda? It's interesting—not knowing what you're going to find next. You learn things."

"I daresay," Freda grumbled. "You get sore feet, too. And there's nowhere for a nice sit down."

But in the end he got his way and we started trundling along street after street, with everything getting less and less green and more and more dingy. There weren't many animals around, either. And the ones that we did meet all seemed to be going the other way. Once, we met a flock of sheep, all scurrying along jostling one another and not looking where they were going. "What's the hurry?" I said, but the sheep just rolled their eyes and all bleated together some stuff about it being best not to go that way. You couldn't get any sense out of them. There didn't seem to be anything wrong with the place, apart from it being dirty and rather dull so far. Offa got into conversation with a flock of starlings and asked them why there were so few animals around, but they just chattered about there being plenty of dogs, and it not being their business and not wanting anything to do with it, until he got bored with them and left them alone. Starlings are just a lot of old gossips, endlessly repeating what they've heard other people say.

Offa was quite right about Manchester. The buildings got bigger and bigger and there were lots of shops, some of them still full of the things the People used. It's amazing how many different kinds of things they had to have. We wandered through some of these, with Stanley picking things up out of the rubbish and rubble everywhere and then dropping them again. He's always wanting to keep what he finds and we have to be very stern about that—no more than will go in his box. He found one place where one of the top floors, that had never been under the water, was full of the clothes that the People used to wear, especially the things some of them wore on their heads, all bright colours and with imitation flowers and fruit on them, and ribbons. He came down with one of these to show us.

"That's nice," said Freda.

"Put it on," said Pansy.

Stanley arranged it on Freda's head, with her horns sticking up through the straw and a bit of veil over one of her eyes. She stood in front of a large mirror, looking at herself. She turned her head this way and that. "Do you think it should be a bit farther back?"

"You look a proper idiot," said Ned, disgusted. "Come on, let's get out of here." He barged into a rail of flimsy pink and blue garments, knocking them over and walking through them.

"Just run up and see if there's another one, Stanley dear," said Freda, "with red flowers. I like red."

It took us ages to get her away from there. She wanted to go on wearing the hat but Ned put his foot down. He said he wasn't going around with anyone looking like that.

Stanley was thoroughly enjoying himself. He loves exploring. He swarmed up the sides of buildings and dropped into them through the broken windows and then came popping up somewhere else, saying, "Hey! Come and look here . . . Guess what I've found now!" and so on and so forth. Freda found a park with trees and flowers and said she was stopping there for a bit. Pansy stayed with her. Ned and Stanley and Offa and I went on exploring. Stanley was very taken with a huge building called City

Art Gallery, full of pictures. He spent ages in there and eventually we went in to fetch him out and found him sitting in the middle of an enormous room with a stone floor and pictures hanging on all the walls. Some of them were of People, just their heads staring out gloomily, and some of them were of People fighting each other, and some of them were of People with no clothes on, and some were of hills and rivers and trees or of flowers or of houses and streets, and some were just blobs and lines and squiggles so that you couldn't really tell what they were of at all.

"Well, I'm blowed!" said Ned. "What's all this in aid of, then? Coming, Stanley?"

"In a minute," said Stanley.

"Don't see the point of all this," said Ned. "What did they want to go making pictures of things for? You can see what a tree's like without making a picture of it, or anything else for that matter. Waste of time."

"You can see more of it," said Stanley.

"Eh?"

"Look," said Stanley. He skipped around the room from picture to picture, saying, "Look, this is clever because it makes you see how the sun shining on water makes patterns on it, and this one looks like just an ordinary tree in a field at first and then you see that's got a pattern too, everything goes inwards towards the tree, and that sunset's really . . ."

"That's not a sunset," said Ned. "That's where somebody spilt something."

"It's a sunset," said Stanley.

So we had an argument about that, and one way and another that set us all off looking at the pictures. "Well," said Ned. "You may have a point, young Stanley. But I don't fancy those over there." He nodded towards a whole row of pictures of People. "Horrible lot."

"I don't know . . ." said Stanley. "When you start looking at them, they're all different. They each give you a different feeling."

"You and your feelings," said Ned. But then he found a picture of some horses and we could hardly drag him away from it. "Now that's a nice bit of picture," he kept saying. "Look at that, then! Fine fellows." There were two very shiny horses standing in a field, and underneath some writing in gold that said, "Lord Rotherham's Stallions, by W. Stubbs (1724–1806)". "Very nice," said Ned. "Smashing."

We spent a long time there. Stanley was getting more and more absorbed, and Ned and I were really quite interested by now. Offa had flown up on to one of the windowsills and was having a nap. "That one's better than that one," said Stanley. "And that's the best one I've seen so far. And that one," he said dramatically, "that one's so good it makes me go all shivery in my spine."

"Come off it, Stanley," said Ned. "No need to exaggerate."

We were so absorbed that we didn't take any notice of the barking at first. There were a lot of dogs around somewhere—outside in the street, presumably. And then it came nearer. From inside the building. I looked round and at the same moment a big alsatian appeared in the doorway and stopped dead as it caught sight of us. "Out!" it barked. "Out! Out! Out! Birds out! Horses out!" It stared at Stanley. "Spiders out!"

Stanley chattered with indignation.

"He's not a spider, mate," said Ned. "Not that I could tell you what he *is*. What's all this, then?"

"Out!" barked the alsatian. Some collies appeared behind him, and a labrador, and joined in. The alsatian said to me, "What's your number? Which unit?"

I said, "I don't know what you're on about. I don't like being shouted at."

"All right," said the alsatian. "Deal with you in a minute. The other two out." He began to snap at Ned's heels. The rest of them were snapping and growling too.

"Here!" said Ned. "Cool it, will you?" He kicked out, rather half-heartedly, and caught one of the collies a slight clip on the shoulder. It yelped. "Sorry," said Ned. "You all right?"

The alsatian rushed to the top of the stairs and stood there barking, "Reinforcements! All units report to the Art Gallery! At the double! Intruders! Repeat—intruders!"

I pushed my way through the other dogs and said to him, "Are you raving mad, you lot? What's the matter with you?"

"You're under arrest," said the alsatian. Two of the collies started coming towards us, with their hackles up.

I said, "I'm no such thing. And you keep away or you'll be sorry. And leave that horse alone."

They all started barking again. "Horses out! Cows out! Cats out!"

And then I remembered Freda and Pansy, still in the park. I yelled to Ned, "Come on—we've got to find the others!" And I rushed the dogs, who were pouring into the building now—dozens of them, terriers, poodles, pekes, everything—and went through them before they knew what was happening, with Ned clattering along behind, kicking out when he had to, and Stanley sitting on his back hanging on to his mane. We burst out into the street, and there were dogs dashing around everywhere. Some of them tried to go for Ned but we kept on going, heading for the place where we'd left the others. Once or twice we got confused and took a wrong turning down unfamiliar streets, and then we came swerving round a corner, with Ned slipping and sliding on the pavements, and Offa flying above, and there it was.

There was no one there. No dogs. And no Freda or Pansy either.

4

In which the enemy is routed; Offa explains about north, south, east and west; Stanley faints and we meet the walking stone

We hunted the park for them, and all the streets and buildings round about. There was absolutely no sign. The boat was where we had left it, by the park gates. Offa flew in all directions and he couldn't see them either. He came back and perched on an iron railing and said, "I don't like it. Gone. Vanished. There shall be weeping and gnashing of teeth."

I said, "I must say I'd like to know what's going on here."

The dogs seemed to have disappeared for the moment. We waited around in the park for a while, hoping that Freda and Pansy might turn up. It was getting towards evening, and we felt more and more uncomfortable in that place. Stanley said, "I don't like it here. Nasty. I don't want to be here when it gets dark."

"I'm with you there, mate," said Ned. "Shut-in kind of feeling. Best get out in the country again."

"I wish we knew where the others were. Poor Freda." Stanley was on the edge of tears.

I said, "Look, they've cleared off somewhere. Stands to reason. Got the wind up when they saw those dogs. So

51

there's no point in hanging around here. Let's move off and tomorrow we can start looking for them again.''

We set off, hurrying now, Ned trotting as fast as he could pull the boat. Luckily it was easy going on the streets. Once or twice some dogs came slinking out from alleys and buildings and barked at us, but we took no notice. When we were more or less on the outskirts of the town we stopped in a field where there was a tumbledown shed for shelter. It was pouring with rain now, and cold. We were all miserable and exhausted. We piled into the shed and as we did so something shot out in a hurry. A scruffy little white dog with its tail between its legs.

''Sorry,'' it said. ''Help yourself. Feel free. No offence meant. Glad to be of any use.''

I said, ''Hang on a minute . . .''

''Just off,'' said the dog. ''Don't want to be in the way.''

Clearly, he wasn't one of that mob in the town. We persuaded him to stop a moment and talk, and when he'd calmed down enough to see that we weren't going to do him any harm, we got quite a lot of sense out of him. The dogs had taken over the town completely, he said. They'd driven everything else out—except birds, which they couldn't get at—and spent their time marauding around on the lookout for anyone foolish enough to drift into the place. They were always fighting among themselves, too, he said, and driving each other from one bit of the town to another. ''Ancoats is all collies now,'' he said. ''And the labradors are moving into Salford. Best thing is to keep well away, if you want to stay out of trouble.''

Stanley said, ''Well, I think they're stupid. Even stupider than I am sometimes.''

When the white dog heard about Freda and Pansy he sounded worried. ''I hope they turn up,'' he said. ''Your friends. There've been one or two nasty things happen recently. There were some sheep . . . Well, I won't go on about it. But I hope your friends are all right." He said goodnight, politely enough, and slipped away into the darkness. He kept himself to himself these days, he said: it was the safest thing to do.

We slept badly and in the morning it was still raining. We were very worried about Freda and Pansy, especially Pansy. We thought that Freda would probably be able to look after herself, if they ran into trouble with the dogs, and they might be all right so long as they were able to stick together, but if they got separated . . .

Offa volunteered to go off and look for them again. As he pointed out, the dogs couldn't do him any harm and he'd probably be able to pick up some information from other birds. He flew off as soon as it was light and we didn't see him again for several hours. At last he came back, damp and bedraggled, and looking worried.

"I've found them," he said. "At least I know where they are."

We crowded round to hear. It had taken him some time, apparently. He'd flown all round the town without seeing or hearing anything, and then all the dogs had come pouring out of the buildings and started lining up in the squares and marching around the streets in groups, chanting.

"What for?" said Stanley.

Offa said, "Search me."

"What did they chant?"

"'Ancoats is ours.' 'Hands off Oldham.' That kind of thing."

"They're welcome to it," said Ned. "Far as I'm concerned. Carry on . . ."

He'd watched the dogs for a bit, he said, along with some other pigeons with whom he'd got into conversation, and when he mentioned Freda and Pansy they said, yes, there'd been some rumour about prisoners being taken the day before. It seemed that from time to time the dogs did that, just to amuse themselves, as far as anyone could see. Offa pieced the story together from various pigeons and starlings and it seemed that Pansy had been chased up a tree by a pack of the dogs, and Freda had gone for them and rescued her ("Brave Freda," said Stanley. "Brave, marvellous Freda.") and then the dogs had chased them both for miles around the town until they'd taken refuge in a great big building somewhere. And there, it seemed, the dogs were besieging them.

I said, "Are they all right?"

"Not too bad," said Offa. "Pansy was in rather a state, they said. Freda's in a bad temper, as much as anything. They haven't got any food."

"Where is this place?"

It was about three miles away, in another part of the town, according to Offa. Some kind of great brick building —not a house or a shop—that the People must have used for storing things in. A nasty dirty place, he said, with big doors on one side that the dogs were guarding, and a kind of yard with a street leading to it, and water on the other side.

"Water?" I pricked up my ears.

"A canal."

I said, "Could we get the boat there?"

Offa said yes, we could. We were quite near to the canal where we were now, and if we got the boat on to it we could go straight to this building. We all looked at each other. I said, "And is there a door from the building on to to the canal?"

It seemed that there was. There was a door opening straight on to it, presumably for loading and unloading, and the dogs weren't bothering to guard that because there was nowhere you could go from it, except into the water.

"Or on to a boat," said Ned. "Good thinking, mate. Let's go then."

We found the canal, under Offa's guidance, and got the boat on to it. It didn't have as much current as an ordinary river so Ned walked along the track beside it and pulled the boat, all through the town under bridges and past buildings and railway lines and notices saying MANCHESTER SHIP CANAL. We passed lots of boats— some of them rather like ours only much bigger, with flat bottoms and little houses with windows where ours is just open. Presently Offa said, "Slow up—we're nearly there. Better go ahead and have a word with Freda. The gates of Zion shall be opened, and our enemies' hosts shall be scattered. See you in a minute."

We had already worked out a plan. Offa should warn Freda that we were on our way, and check that there were no dogs around on the canal side of the building. Then, when we'd got the boat alongside, Freda was to charge the doors and break out. Straight on to the boat. Then we'd be off as fast as we could.

We came under a bridge and there was the building, just as Offa had described. There were no dogs to be seen, though we could hear barking from somewhere not very far away. And then we saw Offa come out of a broken window high up in the building. He swooped down low over us and said, "All clear. Thy enemies shall be smitten, and their cities utterly flung down. Freda's all set to go."

And just at that moment a couple of patrolling dogs came on to the bridge. They hadn't seen us, but they would at any minute. Ned was hidden from them just for the moment, by a pillar of the bridge, but in a few seconds they'd see him, and the boat, and have all the rest round before we could do a thing. I looked at Stanley in dismay; he was squatting at the front end of the boat, ready to jump off when we got alongside the building.

"It's no go, Stanley," I said. "Look at those two."

But he'd already seen them and as I spoke he was already on the move. He took a flying leap from the boat on to the parapet of the bridge, right alongside the dogs, and rushed up and down it, chattering at them. "Yoo-hoo!" he said. "Look at me! Bullies! Dogs out! Dogs out! Come and get me, then, stupids! Yah! Boo!"

The dogs nearly jumped out of their skins. They were just a couple of mangy-looking greyhounds. First they backed away hastily and then they stared and made threatening noises at Stanley. They never saw the boat come out under the bridge and glide slowly towards the edge of the canal, or Ned, plodding along trying to make as little noise as possible with his hooves.

Stanley went on skipping up and down the side of the bridge, keeping the dogs distracted. He did everything he knew how to—standing on his hands, hanging on to things by his tail, taunting and teasing the dogs. He had them completely flummoxed. "Here," they kept saying to each other. "Better report this. Better get the commandant," and every time they started to move off Stanley would produce some more antics.

We manoeuvred the boat alongside the building. I nodded to Offa, who popped back into the building again through the window. Then I jumped off the boat while Ned held it steady and peered through a crack in the doors, just in time to see Offa fly down into the darkness inside. A moment later I saw Freda. "Come on, Freda!" I whispered, and stood back.

Luckily the door was fairly rotten. Freda came bursting

56

through it with bits of splintered wood clinging to her horns, and stood for a moment blinking in the light. Pansy shot out after her. "Quick!" I said. "On to the boat!" The breaking of the door had made a tremendous noise and already the pair of dogs on the bridge had switched their attention from Stanley and were rushing around barking and calling their friends. Freda heaved herself on to the boat; Stanley swung down off the bridge and Pansy jumped on board at the same moment; Offa flew out of the building again and Ned set off up the track at a smart trot.

"Oh, Freda," said Stanley. "I am glad to see you! Are you all right, Pansy?"

Poor Pansy was shivering all over; she'd obviously had a nasty experience. Freda seemed fairly calm, except that she was puffing and blowing with indignation and the exertion of breaking down the door. "Those dogs!" she panted. "Just let me get at them! Just let me give them a piece of my mind!" She didn't sound at all like the placid Freda we were used to.

"Look out!" cried Offa. "They're coming!"

The dogs came round the corner of the building and on to the path in a pack, led by the alsatian we'd met yesterday, all barking, "Out! Out! Everybody out!"

"I'll give them out!" panted Freda furiously. "Just let me off the boat!"

I said, "Now then, Freda," but at that moment the leading dogs caught up with Ned and started snapping at his feet. Freda took a flying leap (flying for her, that is, as an animal who normally moved with great deliberation) off the boat and went for them, head down. A labrador was sent spinning into the canal, yelping. Stanley was standing up at the back of the boat hurling the little glass balls out of his box at the dogs; his aim must have been good because

58

several of them dropped out of the pack howling and dashed off with their tails between their legs. Ned caught the alsatian a clip with his hind leg that stopped him, too. The rest hesitated.

"Had enough?" bellowed Freda. "Anyone else got anything to say for themselves?"

The alsatian, his ears back, was snapping orders to the dogs. "Close ranks and withdraw! Enemy routed! Action terminated!"

"I'll give them action," grumbled Freda, clambering on to the boat again. "Nasty lot of yobbos. I never saw such behaviour. And now if nobody minds could we please get out of here to somewhere where there's a nice bit of grass for tea. I told you no good would come of this place."

We found her the lushest and greenest field we could, drowning in buttercups and meadowsweet, and that night we had a celebration, sitting under the stars while Stanley told stories that got wilder and longer and more and more improbable. One of the stories was about the battle with the dogs, and it became more impressive and preposterous with each telling. Stanley had grown wings and swooped down on the dogs like an eagle, and Freda had swelled to three times her usual size and tossed the dogs right out of the town, one by one, and the boat, which Stanley said was now called VICTORY OF THE HEROES, had turned into solid gold and sailed away with us all into the sunset. "Now then, Stanley," said Freda. "It did no such thing, you know that, and it's called QV 66, don't you go on like that or you'll get us all muddled." But Stanley got more and more carried away, and presently he began to sing a song about the battle, or rather a kind of chant, in which we were all things called kings and knights and Freda was the Great Warrior Queen who came down from the sky, and we fought for forty days and forty nights and then lived happily ever afterwards. We all fell asleep during Stanley's song, and had strange dreams in which what Stanley said had happened and what really happened got all mixed up.

As I've said before, we're bad at remembering how things were, which is partly Stanley's fault because he is never satisfied with what has happened but has to go on inventing things about it. As far as I'm concerned, what was, was, and that's all there is to it, which is why I'm putting this down the way it actually happened, before Stanley gets going on it. Once, Stanley said he was going to write it all down. He found one of the People's type-writers and brought it on to the boat and crouched over it for hours, mumbling to himself and poking at the letters. "This is a special kind of book," he said. "It's got big letters on legs for people who aren't very good at reading, to teach them, but if you're a very *good* reader, like me, then you can play about with it—like this—and the letters make marks on bits of paper and . . ."—he got very excited and began to jump up and down, clattering the keys with all four hands—"oh, *I* see what it's really for."

After that he went into one of his most pompous and irritating moods and snapped at anybody who came near him. He crouched over the typewriter, scowling: he was writing a book, apparently. "Do you mind?" he would groan. "One does happen to need absolute peace and quiet, this isn't something just anyone can do, you know—you have to have lots and lots of ideas, like me, and then no one must interrupt you or it interferes with them." He glared at the typewriter and us, and banged and moaned. But the letters kept jamming, and his bits of paper kept getting creased and torn, so that he ripped them out in a temper and threw them away, and eventually QV 66 had a wake of scrumpled white balls. Finally he threw the typewriter overboard: he said it kept having its own ideas and getting him all muddled.

The morning after the battle with the dogs we had a discussion. I thought we ought to do some serious planning —the journey was getting too hit-or-miss for my liking.

"We're not going to any more towns," said Freda, "and that's flat. I'm a bundle of nerves after that place."

"That's right," agreed Ned, "nothing like the country. Grass. Trees, flowers, birds singing and all that. Grass."

"It's boring," said Stanley.

"Got no soul," said Ned, "that's your trouble. Look at that now." He gazed dreamily out over the fields, misty in the early morning sun. "Beautiful. Gives you nice feelings. And them." He waved a hoof at a clump of cowslips. "Smashing little jobs."

Stanley was very annoyed; he's always going on about how sensitive and poetic he is. "I bet I have nicer feelings than you do," he said aggressively. "More of them. More often. About more things."

"Prove it," said Ned. He moved over to the cowslips and began to munch them appreciatively.

This made Stanley even crosser, so that he hopped up and down chattering and shrieking until Freda said, "That'll do, Stanley, that's quite enough. All I was saying is that if you want to go on with this journey then I'm not going through any more places where there are people like that, or I'm not coming."

So Stanley calmed down and apologised to everybody for behaving badly (only he rather overdid the apologies, which usually meant he wasn't very serious about them), and then he sat down and made Freda a daisy-chain out of the cowslips Ned hadn't eaten and hung it round her horns. Freda stared at herself in a puddle. "Very pretty, dear. Thank you. I wish," she went on wistfully, "I'd brought one of those hats we saw in that place in Manchester. Nice to have, that would have been. Just for special occasions."

"We could find another," said Stanley craftily, "in some other town."

"And they sewed fig leaves together," recited Offa, "and made themselves aprons ..." Freda gave him a suspicious look and said she didn't like that kind of talk, and all she meant was that it's nice to be well turned out. Stanley was busy constructing a hat now, out of oak leaves and trails of ivy, and I could see the discussion was getting quite out of hand, so I said, "Which way are we going?" There were distant sounds of barking, which worried me; I didn't want to get involved with those dogs again.

"The voice of him that crieth in the wilderness," squawked Offa. "What about going south?"

"Going what?" I said.

"South," said Offa, waving a wing. "Thataway."

"What's south?"

"Place a bit farther on," said Stanley. "Got lots of hats in it, Freda." He had finished his now and was decorating it with dandelions.

"No," said Offa, "not a place. General direction of places. Like this ..." He flew down from the bush in which he'd been sitting and put two sticks in the shape of a cross, with his foot, and then drew letters at the end of each arm of the cross: N., S., E. and W. "North, south, east and west. Everything that way is north, everything down there is south, and so on. The mountains skipped like rams; and the little hills like young sheep. Alleluia."

"No, dear," said Freda, "because if you turned it round they'd all be upside down. Things don't stay in the same

62

place. It depends which way you're looking."

"There," said Stanley, picking up Offa's cross and turning it round. "Now south's up there."

"No," said Offa. "Depends on the sun. Bit complicated. Sun always gets up the same side every morning; that's east. Goes down opposite; that's west. Similarly north and south."

"Really?" said Ned, interested. "Fancy. I never noticed that. Bright fellow, Offa."

Offa looked away modestly, and Stanley, who doesn't like anyone else to be clever, said loudly that *everyone* knew *that*, it was just too obvious for words. He took a quick look at the sun, and then down at Offa's cross again.

I asked Offa how he knew about all this.

"Picture in a book in the Bishop's Library at Lichfield," he explained. "All about the world being round and that kind of thing. Let there be a firmament in the midst of the waters. Let the earth bring forth grass. Let there be light."

"No, dear," said Freda, "it's flat. You can see that, you've only got to look. You could fall off the edge, that's what I'm always a bit worried about."

"Oh, ye of little faith," said Offa irritably. "It turns round and round, too, and goes round the sun."

"Well, I never!" said Ned. "What's it want to do that for, then?"

Freda said that made her feel all unsettled.

I'm not clever, like Stanley, but I saw all of a sudden that this might be useful, knowing this stuff about the sun, and which direction was what. I said, "Is London north or south or east or west?"

"Don't know," said Offa sadly.

Stanley was sitting with his back to us now, sulking. He didn't like Offa stealing the limelight like this. He'd found an apple and was throwing it up and down and catching it. "If it goes round and round," he said, "why don't we fall off it, then, when it's upside down?" He looked at Offa triumphantly.

"Search me," said Offa, "I only got up to chapter three. Should have read more. Have to go back to Lichfield and find out."

Stanley threw his apple around a bit more, higher and higher, and then sat down and looked at it. He'd gone all thoughtful. "Why doesn't it go on up into the sky?" he said suddenly.

"Things just don't, dear, do they?" said Freda, eyeing the apple. "Were you wanting that, Stanley? It would make a nice little snack before we go."

Stanley swarmed up the tree we were sitting by and started pulling apples off it and hurling them down. "There!" he shouted. "And there! And there, and there and there! Why don't they go upwards? That's what I want to know." He jumped up and down on the branch, excitedly. "Why don't I go upwards? Why don't we all go upwards?"

"Thank you, dear," said Freda, munching. "Very nice. A bit unripe, some of them."

"Can't know the answers to everything, young Stanley," said Ned, joining Freda among the apples.

"Oh, you're stupid, all of you," said Stanley. He somersaulted off the tree and stamped around in the apples, throwing them at the branches.

I said, "Never mind all that. I think we ought to be getting on. South, then, like Offa suggested."

So we went south.

There were always plenty of animals about: horses, cows, sheep, cats, dogs, all the small fry by way of rabbits, mice, squirrels and so forth. Lots of birds. Foxes from time to time; the odd herd of deer; now and again something a bit out of the ordinary like a donkey or a snake or a stoat. Of course everyone stares at Stanley and a lot of them make remarks of one kind or another. Stanley says he's so used to it he doesn't take any notice; which isn't entirely true. Once, after some bullocks had been gawping at him and saying some pretty silly things he went off and hid in a bush. It took us hours to coax him out again. When at last he did emerge he said pathetically, "Do you think I'm a mistake?"

"No, of course not," said Freda. "I think someone worked you out very nicely. It was very clever to think of having a tail you can hold on to things with." She swished hers around experimentally.

Pansy said, "If you are a mistake you're ever such a nice one."

I told Stanley not to take any notice of the bullocks and suchlike. "Just you wait, we'll find someone else like you in London."

"Are you sure?" said Stanley, brightening up.

"Sure," I said firmly. I wasn't really, but you don't get anywhere by being pessimistic.

It was a few days after we left Manchester that we found the walking stone. At least Pansy found it. She had been rummaging around under a hedge, after mice or something, and came wandering out and said, "There's a stone in there that's got feet. It walks about."

"Let's have a look," said Stanley. He went diving into the hedge and was in there for half a minute, and then he came bursting out and collapsed on to his back with his eyes closed. After nobody had taken any notice for another minute he sat up and said, "I've just fainted, if anyone's interested."

"Yes, dear," said Freda. "We saw."

And then there was an upheaval in the hedge and a part of it crawled out on to the grass. More precisely, a large, oval stone with a lot of leaves and twigs stuck to it and four scaly legs, one at each corner, and a flat scaly head. Stanley shot up into a tree and said, "There! Told you so!"

"Well, blow me down!" said Ned. We all gathered round and stared at the stone. I sniffed it. The four legs and the head immediately vanished.

"Wotcha," said Ned. "How do. Anyone at home?"

The stone put out the tip of its nose, cautiously, and peered at us. Then it said, "I don't suppose you've got such a thing as a banana about you?"

"A what?" said Ned.

"Banana," said the stone. When none of us responded it went on irritably, "Long yellow thing. Curved. Very good eating. Or dates, for that matter? No? I don't know," it said with a sigh, "you just can't seem to lay your hands on them nowadays. Time was, they were all over the place. Now it's nothing but dandelions, dandelions, dandelions . . ." It heaved another sigh and went on, looking at Stanley, "I should think you miss them, too. I've seen your friends and relations having a good tuck in."

We all pricked up our ears. "What?" said Stanley, creeping closer. The stone was turning itself round now, rather cumbrously, and heading back into the hedge.

"Hang on a minute," I said.

"Sorry," said the stone. "Haven't got time. Going to sleep again."

"Oh, please," said Stanley, "*where* did you see my friends and relations? *When?*"

The stone stopped and heaved itself round again and stared at him. "Don't ask me. Never been any good at names and dates. Except the kind you eat."

66

It was Pansy who put into words what we'd all been thinking, and not liking to say. "What are you?" she said.

The stone groaned. "The ignorance of people . . . Only last year someone asked me that. Or was it the year before? Tortoise, child, tortoise. *Testudinae*. Seychelles tortoise, to be precise. Female. Purchased 1924. Please do not feed."

Stanley said, "Have you really seen animals like me?"

The tortoise peered up at him out of its little black eyes and said testily, "Said I had, didn't I? Don't ask me details, though. When a person gets to be a few hundred years old time ceases to have much meaning. One year's much the same as another. All I know is once there were bananas and now there aren't. And they talk about progress . . ." It began to shuffle off again.

"Where were they?" said Stanley desperately.

"In the next cage," said the tortoise, disappearing now into the hedge. "Or was that the South American condor? Either that or the aviary. 'Bye for now. See you at the millennium."

We watched it vanish into the undergrowth. "Well!" said Freda. "Anyway, you're not the only thing there's only one of, Stanley, that's some consolation."

Pansy said, "You're much prettier than it was, too, Stanley." She wandered off and stared at herself in a puddle, complacently. Pansy is very vain.

Stanley sat in a morose little bundle, gazing into the hedge, his large black eyes filled with tears (he cries very easily). Occasionally a tear plopped down his face and he would sniff and wipe it away with the back of his hand. "It might have *said*," he muttered. "It might have just *concentrated* a bit."

"There now, Stanley old son," said Ned. "Pull yourself together. Stiff upper lip and all that. Have a mushroom."

It was ages before we could persuade him to leave the

hedge, and then only after some sparrows had assured him that the tortoise only woke up every few months, and that for a few minutes at a time. "I'm not stopping here for months," said Freda, "and that's flat." So at last we got him to move on, reluctantly. He cheered himself up navigating QV 66 by the sun, according to what Offa had said about it getting up in the east and going down in the west. ("Of course," he said, "one always *knew* that—it's just that one had kind of forgotten about it just lately.") He sat at the back on his bicycle saddle, with his box of precious things and the *Shorter Oxford English Dictionary* beside him, and his oak and ivy leaf hat on his head, squinting into the sky and making a great fuss about steering and how difficult it was and how expert you had to be. He made up a song about the south being a place where the sun shone all the time and everyone was happy and there were people like him everywhere. "Let us come unto the gates of Jerusalem!" squawked Offa. "Hosanna! You want to watch out for that log, there, Stanley—left a bit . . ."

5

In which we pass through Birmingham, are concerned with football and beefburgers and peacocks, Ned wins by a length and a half, and Stanley goes swimming because he never could tell left from right

We drifted here and there for a long time. We would lose the particular road we had been trying to follow, because it suddenly plunged into the water, and then would be unable to pick it up again and wander around for days trying to find another sign pointing to London. It was around then that we came to the place called Derby which cast doubt upon Ned's claims about his ancestors. Often we found that London seemed to be getting farther, rather than nearer, according to the road signs, and realised that we had changed direction.

We reached a point where all the roads were signposted BIRMINGHAM. Stanley did some thinking and had a short headache and announced that that probably meant it was a big place.

"Why?" said Freda.

"Because otherwise they wouldn't have bothered telling everyone how to get there."

"Perhaps it was just a very nice place," said Freda, "with lots of grass and room to sit down."

"They didn't eat grass," said Stanley. "At least I don't

69

think they did. I wonder what they did eat?" We had never thought about that before.

"Mice, I expect," said Pansy.

"Don't be silly. There wouldn't have been enough."

"What's there most of?" said Pansy.

We thought for a moment. "Sheep," I said. I looked at Freda, and then away again, quickly. Pansy said, "There's lots of cows, too."

There was a silence and then Freda said in a horrified voice, "You don't think they . . . ?"

I've always thought it pretty pointless to harp on things that are unpleasant; there usually isn't anything you can do about them anyway. The world isn't an altogether nice place and some nasty things happen, but one must just get on and make the best of it. Stanley doesn't agree; he says you ought to scream and howl and at least you've shown what you feel about it then. But I didn't see any point in dwelling on the People and their habits, so I said briskly that I thought it would be a good idea if Offa flew on a bit and had a look at Birmingham and came back and told us what it was like.

"Right you are," said Offa. "Will do."

He was gone all day. When he got back he was very disparaging about the place. "Enormous," he said. "Miles and miles of it—buildings and factories and shops and what have you. It hasn't even got a cathedral," he went on in disgust. "Not a single really high-class roost to be seen. Trouble is, it's right in the way. If we want to go on going south, we've got to go round it, or through it. There's not a lot of water. We could," he said thoughtfully, "go over it. They've got roads on legs down there, on kind of stalks, lifted up above everything else, going in all directions. It would be easy going for the boat along those."

And so we trundled through Birmingham—or rather

above it—on the People's roads. It took days and days, and Ned and Freda became very petulant about the lack of grass. We had to keep stopping for them to graze at places alongside the roads that Stanley thought the People used for eating at ("Eating what?" said Freda suspiciously) during their journeys. They had huge rooms full of tables and chairs and notices saying things like Beefburger & Chips 40p., Sausage, Egg & Chips 35p., Steak, Chips & Salad 80p. Freda made Stanley read them to her.

"I don't know why," she said, "but I get a funny feeling in these places. I feel creepy. What does Beefburger mean? And Sausage?"

"I don't know," said Stanley, "it doesn't matter anyway," and he went off to play with one of the machines. He loved the machines. Most of them were rusted up and broken, but there were some that still worked—machines with buttons you pressed that made numbers pop up behind, and one with rows of little People on sticks that went round and round when you twiddled the sticks. "What's it for?" said Ned, staring. "It's to make them dance," said Stanley. "Look," and he twiddled the knobs at the end of the stick and the figures spun round and round. "I think it's to make them kick a ball into those nets at the ends of fields," said Ned, "like in that picture up there, see?" and Stanley stared at a picture on the wall showing People rushing around a green field kicking a ball, and then back at the machine. "Oh," he said, and then, "Oh, I see . . ." After that it took us hours to get him away. He wanted to take the machine with us but Ned wasn't having any of that.

Sometimes there were books in those places, with bright shiny pictures on the covers, and piles of newspapers. "Ugh!" said Ned, trampling through the papers. "Nasty-looking lot, weren't they?" He put his hoof through a large picture called MISS BLACKPOOL 1977. "Grinning away like a lot of loonies; ugly as sin."

"I don't think that's very nice," said Freda. "No one can help their personal appearance, can they? We'll go somewhere else now, if you don't mind. What's that, I'd like to know?" She was gazing at a machine with a picture of a cow on it, labelled ICE-COLD MILK 10p. "I don't care for these places, not one bit."

We got past Birmingham at last, and into country again. A good deal of it was under water still, but the water was mostly shallow, and any higher ground was pretty dry. It was fortunate that QV 66 was quite flat-bottomed, or we would have got stuck even more often than we did. As it was, we got along pretty well, meandering past hedges and woods, with Ned and Freda squelching along-side and Freda complaining about how she was going to catch her death if she had to go on much longer like this with wet feet day in day out. We seriously considered abandoning the boat, now that the water was going down so fast, but then Offa did some exploratory flying on ahead and reported that there was a good wide river that we could put QV 66 on to, at a place called Warwick where two rivers joined up. "Decent little place," he said. "Couple of rather spectacular roosts—biggish church, not cathedral-size but not bad, and a castle."

So we headed for Warwick. After a bit we struck the river, and were able to get QV 66 properly afloat. Offa was quite right: it was an excellent river, wide and deep, and it led us straight to the town one fine sunny morning, so that we came round a bend and saw this great stone building that Offa said was the castle, floating all golden above the river mist. "That's nice," said Freda, "very pretty. I like that. Ever so important-looking."

We tied QV 66 up beside a bridge and got out to explore
the castle. There was a great deal of it—enormous rooms
and towers with twisting staircases and nasty dark damp
underground places and great high walls towering above
the river. There was a nice grassy place all round it, too,
that Freda and Ned enjoyed, except for the presence of
some very odd birds such as we had never seen before,
with enormous blue and green tails that they could open
up and spread out. Proper show-offs, they were, marching
up and down opening and shutting their tails at us, and
screeching in the most horrible high-pitched voices. "Oh,
shut up, will you," said Ned irritably.

"Look at us!" screeched the birds. "Admire the iri-
descence of our feathers! Marvel at our incomparable
design! We are the most beautiful creatures in existence!"

"No, you're not," said Freda, "you're a bit vulgar if you ask me. Overdone."

Stanley rushed off into the castle, reappearing from time to time in a state of happy excitement at the things he'd found. He produced a long sharp metal stick with a handle at one end in the shape of a cross, and made howling noises as he brandished it around. "It was for killing People with," he explained. "It's called a sword."

"What!" said Freda, horrified. "You mean they killed each other?"

"Must've done," said Stanley. He rushed up on to the castle walls with the sword and waved it around at imaginary enemies, taking great leaps from one tower to another, and up and down flights of stairs. "Ha!" he yelled. "Have at you! Got yer! Avaunt! A hit! A hit!" "Be careful, dear," said Freda. "You don't want to fall off there, you could do yourself a nasty injury." Stanley vanished round a corner, whooping. He came back from an investigation of the inside of the castle with a round gold hat which he said was called a crown. Freda liked it very much and wore it over one horn for the rest of the day.

"All the same," she said, as we left the castle, "I didn't care for that place. I think they had some nasty habits, the People. Sticking those things into each other." She glanced at Stanley's sword with distaste. "And you're not taking that thing with you, not if I have anything to do with it."

Stanley seemed as though he was about to protest, and then dropped the sword into the river. "I was only pretending with ,it," he said regretfully. Freda was still looking stern, though the effect was spoiled by the crown which made her look somewhat absurd.

"*I* only kill things if I want to eat them," said Pansy piously.

"That's nasty too," snapped Freda. She can be very disapproving of other people's way of life.

"It's her nature," said Stanley, in his most earnest manner. "Like it's my nature to be good at having ideas. And like I'm more sensitive than other people."

Freda sniffed. Ned broke in to say that he didn't think it was on, really, to go round poking other blokes with sharp things but what did you do if they'd done it to you first and you'd asked them to push off but they wouldn't? I thought he had a point there. We were still arguing about it as we walked up into the town.

It was quite a small town, and because it was on a hill it had never been under the water and so the buildings were full of interesting things for Stanley. He vanished for ages into one called Public Library and when I went inside to find him he was sitting hunched over a book in the middle of a whole pile of books he'd been pulling down from the shelves. He was very cross at being interrupted and said he'd found the longest poem in the world and it was all about these two People who lived in a beautiful garden and got thrown out of it for eating the wrong kind of tree. "They were a bit stupid," he said thoughtfully. "I wouldn't have done that. I'd have guessed you shouldn't and eaten something else instead." He insisted on taking the book with him and another which he said he was going to read to us in the evenings. It was called *The Collected Works of William Shakespeare*. "It's good," he said. "There's this story in it about a person called Hamlet who's very sensitive and miserable. Actually," he went on, "he's rather like me."

I couldn't get him to come out so eventually I left him and went off to do some more exploring of my own in some houses at the edge of the town where there was an interesting colony of rats. I had a nice time exercising them and came back a couple of hours later to find quite a crowd in the middle of the town, just outside the big church —bullocks and cats and dogs and a crowd of starlings lining the rooftops, gossiping to each other and commenting on something that was going on out of sight. "What's up?" I asked one of the bullocks.

"There's some barmy type climbed up the front of the church," he said, "making a speech or something."

I sighed, and pushed through the crowd. Stanley was sitting on an arched ledge high up almost in the tower of the church, waving his arms about and reciting in a loud voice. "Can't understand a word of it," grumbled the bullocks. "What's he on about?" Some animals, on the other hand, were rather impressed. "It sounds ever so nice," said a tabby cat, gazing up at Stanley. "Not that I altogether follow what he's saying, mind." "Who does he think he is?" asked a spaniel indignantly. "Very pretentious, I call it."

Freda appeared round a corner and bellowed indignantly, "Stanley! You come down at once!" Stanley, interrupted in full stream, looked down and wavered a bit on his ledge. "Stanley!" said Freda sternly.

Stanley slithered down from ledge to ledge until he arrived on the ground again. "Stop showing off," said Freda.

Stanley said in injured tones, "I wasn't showing off. I was just telling them my poem."

I pointed out that it wasn't his poem, since somebody called Milton had made it up in the first place: Stanley was still holding the book and I could see the writing on the outside. "Well, I'm making it better, aren't I?" he said. "I'm putting in a few new bits of my own—some of it wasn't all that good."

"That'll do, anyway," said Freda. "You should think of

other people. It's very embarrassing being associated with someone who will keep on making an exhibition of himself.''

''Phooey,'' said Stanley rudely.

We managed to get him away through the crowd of animals, who were now beginning to pass remarks about him, most of which were uncomplimentary. ''Savages,'' said Stanley with disdain. ''Peasants.'' He swaggered through them with his books tucked under one arm. ''Some people,'' he said, ''are quite incredibly un-cultivated.''

''Knowledge puffeth up, but charity edifieth,'' rumbled Offa, flying down from a chimney-pot. ''Anyone seen Ned?''

We looked at each other, and realised that nobody had, not since we left the castle, which was some time ago now. We began to hunt the streets for him. Offa flew about all over the place, without success. It was late afternoon and would be dark before all that long. We wanted to get back to the boat before then.

''I don't know,'' Freda kept saying worriedly, ''it isn't like him at all.'' We wandered all around the town, calling. No Ned. Offa decided to look farther afield, and flew off while the rest of us searched houses and shops and the church and a great open-sided building full of rusty cars. There was no sign of Ned anywhere. And then Offa reappeared, triumphant but anxious, to say that he'd found him. ''Quite near,'' he said. ''Kind of great big field place with a lot of fences, just on the edge of the town. Got a sign saying Warwick Racecourse.''

''Well, that's all right, then,'' said Freda. ''Tell him to come back.''

''He won't listen,'' said Offa in a worried tone. ''He's behaving very oddly. I think you'd better come.''

So we followed him, and sure enough, there was Ned just as he had said, walking round and round a small circular field with a white fence round it and a notice saying JOCKEYS AND TRAINERS ONLY. At least he wasn't so much walking as fidgeting. He pranced for a few paces, and then did a kind of sideways jig, and then danced around in a circle neighing. He didn't seem to be at all himself.

"Ned," said Freda, "it's time to go back to the boat."

Ned jigged towards us and looked down his nose at her. "Flying Warrior, if you don't mind. Three minutes till the start now and I'm five to one on. See you later."

He dashed suddenly towards the gate and out on to the grass beyond, where he started cantering off in a crabwise fashion, with his head flung back, occasionally kicking. We watched in amazement. When he arrived at a line of some kind of large metal boxes in the distance he shuffled into one of them, with much neighing and rearing around, and then came bursting out again at a gallop. He galloped flat out past us and then away into the distance, getting, I must say, appreciably slower all the time. We lost sight of him and then suddenly he reappeared from the opposite direction, lumbering now rather than galloping, and covered with sweat. He came to a stop at last not far away, and crawled back to us, steaming like an autumn mist.

"I won," he panted. "Length and a half."

I said, "Ned, have you gone completely mad?"

He squinted blearily at me and said, "Flying Warrior. Either you call me Flying Warrior or I'm stopping here." He was blowing so much that he could hardly speak and looked as if he might collapse at any minute. Freda was fussing away over him and saying he could strain himself rushing about like that, and he'd catch his death of cold, getting that overheated. Ned said dreamily, "Came up from behind, I did, back in the straight—one minute I was lying seventh and then would you believe it I was out in front with no one else in the running. Fantastic!"

We managed to persuade him to come away, and returned to the boat, all six of us, just as it was getting dusk. We settled down for the night in a field beside the river, with QV 66 tied up to the bridge nearby, and fell asleep with Stanley reading us a long boring story from his Shakespeare book. He must have fallen asleep over it himself, eventually, because in the morning he was lying curled up with the book on top of him.

Ned was so stiff he could hardly move. "There!" said Freda, "I told you so!" He gave her a surly look and staggered gingerly around the grass. "Ouch!" he said. "Oooh! Aah! I'm not pulling that boat today, and that's for sure."

Fortunately there was no need. The river was wide, deep and fast. Stanley was in one of his most bouncy moods. He had found a large piece of iron and decided to make it part of the boat's steering system. He spent a good deal of time fiddling about with it and explaining how it worked to anyone who would listen. "It's really quite simple," he said, "so simple in fact that only a very clever person would have thought of it." He squatted on the bank, admiring what he had done, and went on, "It's really very odd, but you have to be specially brilliant to see the easiest way of doing something. Now, most people wouldn't have seen how to fix that on to there. How would you have fixed that on to there, Pansy?"

"I wouldn't have," said Pansy.

"Quite," said Stanley. He strutted around the back of the boat, ostentatiously testing the wind by holding up a feather, and squinting at the sun. "Actually I've invented a new system of navigating today, too. Nobody's ever thought of it before. It works like this . . ."

"Well, let's get on with it then, young Stanley," said Ned. He began ambling along the river bank, with Freda a little way behind. Pansy jumped on to the boat. I was already on it, having a doze in the sun. Offa was chatting to some friends of his in a big tree beside the bridge. Stanley cast off and we drifted under the bridge, and along towards the castle, rather fast—there had been a lot of rain and the river was full to the brim with a strong current flowing. Stanley was standing importantly at the back of the boat, clutching the piece of iron, which was now the handle of the steering gear. "Mind out," he bawled at a couple of swans, who paddled off indignantly. "Make way, you small craft. Keep clear."

Suddenly there was a cry of alarm from Offa, who had flown up to the castle ramparts. "Keep right," he called. "There's a weir coming up. Keep right, Stanley."

"What?" said Stanley.

"A weir." Offa came flapping down and circled over-head, sounding more and more agitated. "River all falling down over a cliff. Smash the boat up. Go *right*."

We could see, now, that the river forked just ahead, and there was indeed a disturbing noise of rushing, falling water. Stanley yanked at his piece of iron, and QV 66 began to turn left.

"No, no," cried Offa. "The other way. That's left."

"No, it isn't," said Stanley, "I know about left and right. I'm an expert about left and right." He steered harder still to the left.

We've had these arguments before, ever since Stanley first discovered about left and right from road signs. He was immensely pleased with himself, and from then on he's always got them wrong.

"Just leave this to me," said Stanley. "The great thing in this kind of situation is to keep absolutely calm. Just keep your head, and you'll be quite all right. Here we go . . ." He hauled wildly at the steering gear and QV 66, now almost under the left bank, where Ned and Freda were trotting around anxiously, hit the fastest bit of the current and began to rush headlong towards the line of white, broken water which, I suddenly saw, marked the edge of the weir.

Stanley saw it at the same moment. "Help!" he shrieked. "Help! Somebody do something!" He gave the piece of iron another heave and it came off in his hands and tipped him on to his back in the bottom of QV 66. He jumped up again and dashed frantically up and down. "Help! Save us! Ned! Freda! Stop the river! Oh, I'm stupid, I'm hopeless—somebody do something."

The weir was only a few yards ahead now. "Jump!" called Offa. "All of you! Stanley! Pal! Pansy!."

I jumped for the bank, missed, fell backwards into the water, paddled like mad for the bank again, heaved myself out, and looked round just in time to see QV 66 go upended down over the weir, with Stanley and Pansy clinging on to one side.

6

In which QV 66 is repaired, the voyage proceeds to Oxford by way of Stratford, Stanley invents music and Pansy goes flying by mistake

We rushed to the bank at the foot of the weir. QV 66 had crashed down sideways, turned right over, and was now floating away upside down, with a hole in the bottom and part of one side torn away. There was no sign of either Stanley or Pansy.

"Woe! Woe!" wailed Offa. "By the waters of Babylon we sat down and wept . . ."

And then a string of bubbles began to move rapidly towards the bank, getting larger and larger. All of a sudden the bubbles became a small, dark, bedraggled object which crawled out on to the bank and collapsed wetly on the grass.

It was Stanley. We crowded round him.

"You all right, Stanley, old son?" said Ned.

"Slurp," said Stanley, coughing water all over the place. "Brr! . . . Hic . . ."

There was a faint mewing noise from behind us. We turned round, and saw Pansy, soaking wet, clutching a small plank which was spinning in the current. The plank was swallowed for a moment by an eddy, and Pansy with it. When she bobbed up again she looked more dead than alive. "Help!" she said faintly. We looked at each other, aghast.

Stanley had staggered to his feet. "I swam," he said weakly. "It's easy. You just . . ."

"Help!" mewed Pansy. The plank lurched and nearly turned over again.

"Oh dear," mooed Freda. "Can't somebody do something? You hold on tight, Pansy dear, we're coming to get you."

I looked at the river. It was fast and deep and dark. "Right," I thought, and then, "No, I can't . . ." And then, again, "Right. *Now*." Pansy, spinning round and round in circles, was drifting rapidly away.

There was a splash beside us. "Ouch!" gasped Stanley, disappearing into the water and then re-emerging again, just his head and flailing arms. "Help! Cold! Coming, Pansy."

"Good old Stanley," said Ned admiringly. "Well, I never!"

Stanley vanished, blowing bubbles. He popped up again and spluttered, "It's really quite easy, all you have to do is . . .", and then disappeared under a raft of drifting weed. "Help!" he said, reappearing for an instant. "Not sure if I . . ." We lost sight of him again. Moments later something dark and struggling surfaced for a moment and squeaked, "Having a bit of a problem with . . ." There was a swirl and it disappeared again.

"Oh dear," said Freda anxiously. "Is he going to be all right?"

Amid a frenzied splashing alongside Pansy's plank Stanley's head appeared and then his hands clutching at the plank. "No," he gasped. "Got a better idea. Hang on a minute." There was some more plunge and splash, while

Pansy mewed pathetically, clinging on for dear life, and then the curled, snake-like end of Stanley's tail appeared and hooked itself around the log. "Need hands for swimming," he explained, taking a mouthful of water at the same time. "Got to . . ." The rest of the sentence trailed off in a kind of gargling noise. He set off for the bank, rather more stylishly, though still vanishing under the water from time to time, with the plank, firmly held by his tail, following behind, Pansy aboard.

He heaved himself on to the bank, and after him the shivering and dejected Pansy.

"Stanley," I said, "that was pretty good. Really rather impressive."

"Mighty above all things," agreed Offa. "Hail! Hosanna!"

We dried Pansy off with grass and leaves and warmed them both up. Pansy said, "It was dreadful. It was the most dreadful thing that has ever happened to me. Thank you *ever* so much, Stanley. I think you're wonderful." (But in ten minutes, I should point out, she had forgotten all about it and was playing in some dead leaves with a beetle she had found.)

Stanley, his teeth still chattering, said graciously, "That's quite all right, Pansy, don't mention it." He looked round at us. "Did you see that fancy stuff I was doing at the end? That was a special swimming style I'd just invented."

"It was very clever, dear," said Freda.

"Swimming," explained Stanley, "and all those kind of things—running and jumping and flying—do you remember that time I went flying?—they're all just a matter of keeping your head and being very brave and calm. And of course being very good at it, like me."

Ned said, "Let's have another dekko at that fancy stroke, Stanley."

Stanley glanced at the river. There was a pause and then he said, "Actually it's very important not to overdo things like swimming. Even when you're very good at it you should only do a little at a time, or it's bad for you."

"Ah," said Ned, "I see."

"And anyway," said Stanley, "we ought to be getting on."

We all remembered QV 66 at the same moment. It had drifted some way down the river and was lodged against the bank now under some overhanging trees, upside-down. We hurried to inspect the damage. It was a depressing sight. Apart from the hole in the bottom, a good part of one side had been ripped away, so that it would let water in there also, and Stanley's steering gear had vanished completely, along with the bicycle seat, his books and his box of precious things. We looked at each other in gloom. "My books," wailed Stanley, "my tools . . ."

And at that same moment I spotted the box wedged up against some driftwood farther downstream. Stanley rushed off and was able to drag it ashore. Some of the things were rather wet, but he spread the books out to dry in the sun, and found that his tools were all right. He began to cheer up.

I said, "Can you mend it?" Meaning, of course, the boat.

Stanley scurried up and down, poking at the broken planks and the hole in the bottom. Then he said, "Yes, I think so. Might take a bit of time. Better get going. Nails," he went on energetically, "lots of them. Bits of wood. Probably find some up in the town. Let's go."

It took several days. There were times when Stanley despaired and crawled away to lie under a bush with a headache. "I'm stupid," he moaned. "Hopeless. Clumsy. Useless." And then a few hours later he'd come bursting out and set to again with a hammer and nails and saw, ordering everyone around and bouncing up and down the boat, which had been dragged out on to the grass by Ned and lay bottom up surrounded by Stanley's paraphernalia of wood and tools. But at last he did finish it.

"Stanley," said Ned, "you are a genius, and that's a fact."

"Mmn . . ." said Stanley, with his head on one side, studying the boat. He seemed dissatisfied. "Hang on a bit," he said, and went scampering off in the direction of the town. He reappeared an hour or two later clutching some tins and a large brush.

By the end of the day the boat was bright red, and so was a good deal of Stanley. He kept sending us up into the town to hunt for more of these tins of paint, and when the red ran out he changed to black and green and blue and improved on things with decoration and pictures. He rewrote the name in huge white letters—QV 66 PROPERTY OF THE PORT OF LONDON AUTHORITY RETURN TO DEPOT 3. ("What does it mean?" asked Pansy, and Stanley said, "I don't know, but it sounds nice and important.") Freda was a bit doubtful. She said, "Isn't it a bit conspicuous now, dear? You don't want things to stand out too much."

"Yes, you do," said Stanley, and he gave QV 66 two enormous eyes at the front, so that it could see where it was going. And he stuck a pole up at one end and tied on to it a huge piece of coloured material—red, white and blue stripes—that he had taken off a pole on top of a building in Warwick. "There!" he said with satisfaction. "That's more like it."

Freda, however, continued to be embarrassed by the appearance of the boat.

We set off once more. Since the river seemed to be heading in the right direction we kept QV 66 on it and drifted downstream, reaching another town after a very short while, called Stratford. As usual, Stanley insisted on stopping to explore, so we tied up at another bridge and Stanley had a great deal of fun in a huge building nearby where there were hundreds and hundreds of seats in rows facing a bare, wooden floor. "*I* know what this place is for," he said. "You lot have to sit out there in those seats and watch me pretending to be things I'm not."

"Why?" said Freda. "What would we want to do that for?"

"For *fun*," said Stanley crossly. And he pranced around waving his arms and reciting bits out of his book. He strutted about and pretended to fight people and lay down and cried and generally made an exhibition of himself. Freda watched sourly. "What are you doing that for?" she said.

"I'm being a king leading an army into battle," he shouted furiously. "Can't you *see*?"

"Not really," said Freda. "You look like you, to me. Whatever you are."

Stanley swarmed up some steps at one side and made faces at her from a window at the top. "Nobody understands me," he complained. "One is absolutely on one's own. There simply isn't anyone who knows how one feels."

"Oh, come off it, Stanley," said Ned. "Time to be moving on, anyway."

We left Stratford, and a mile or so farther down the river Offa announced that he thought it was going in the wrong direction. He'd been picking up information from other birds and they all seemed pretty convinced that that particular river wouldn't take us south, and furthermore the road signs saying London were all pointing a different way. So we hauled the boat off the river, and Stanley did some repair work on the wheels, and we set off by land once more, with Ned grumbling a bit at having to do some work.

"I wasn't bred for this kind of thing," he said. "Carthorse stuff. Come from a long line of winners, I do. I'm demeaning myself."

We travelled through much countryside with nothing bigger than small villages full of tumbledown stone houses, and after some time we found ourselves on the outskirts of a big town again. It was called Oxford. Offa flew off to have a look at it and came back greatly excited. "Very superior place," he said. "Really high-class. Full of churches and buildings pretty well on cathedral-scale. Very nice indeed. O Jerusalem, Jerusalem!"

"It says Oxford," said Ned, "not Jerusalem." But Offa had already flown off again.

We trundled down wide roads into this place, and indeed, as he had promised, it was quite impressive as towns go, full of huge buildings with towers and spires. There was one place that Freda particularly admired, with great pillars and carved things around the top, and a big flight of steps up to the doors. We went inside and found rooms upon rooms with bits of china in glass cases, and pictures, and a lot of other things in glass cases, and statues of People with no clothes on, most of them partly broken. "I wonder what they were for?" said Freda, staring. "I can't see the point, personally."

We wandered on and came to a room with more glass cases in which were strange wooden things with rows of strings, and long wooden objects with a lot of shiny metal keys and buttons. Freda wondered what they were for, too. "Tools," said Stanley, "old-fashioned kind of tools. Before the People invented hammers and saws and things like I've got they used things like this. Actually they were for magicking, too, what you did was . . ." I said I thought he was wrong, and pointed out a painting on the wall showing People using some of the wooden things. "The

Music-making", it was called. Stanley's eyes opened very wide. "*Oh*," he said.

One of the glass cases was labelled "Violin (Le Meissie). Maker: Antonio Stradivari". Stanley broke the glass and took the violin out. He held it like the People in the picture and stroked it with the stick that was beside it. There was an unpleasant high-pitched squeak. Freda shot backwards, her hooves clattering on the stone floor. "Do you mind . . ." she mooed. "That noise goes right through my head." Stanley, however, insisted on taking the violin with him. "It's got possibilities," he explained, "once I can get the hang of it."

We toured the town. Freda found herself a rather unbecoming square black hat in a shop and wore it for a bit until it fell off, and Stanley brought her a bright scarlet hood which she wore also for a while until she said it was making her hot. From time to time we saw Offa strutting contentedly around the ledge of a tower or a spire, cooing about the temples of the ungodly and the pillars of Zion. "Nice to see the lad happy," said Ned. "We might stop here a day or two."

And so we did. Stanley fell through a broken grating in the pavement and discovered what he claimed were enormous underground caves full of books. "Actually all the books in the world were kept here," he said, "millions of them. One day I'm going to come back here and read them all, but I haven't got time just now." He also spent a lot of time playing about with his violin, and the noises that he made with it became gradually a little less unbearable. They were organised, as you might say: some thought had gone into what noise came after what other noise. Stanley sat there scraping away, hour after hour, very pleased with himself. "Nice, isn't it?" he said casually, "It's called music. I've just invented it."

"Hmm . . ." said Ned, "I daresay you could get a taste for it, given time." He took himself off out of earshot.

It was not long after that that we found the shop with all the toys in it: very small trains and cars and models of People doing various things we couldn't understand. There were models of animals, too, which we thought stupid-looking. Stanley found a creature that looked rather like him and threw it out of the window in disgust. He pottered around therefor ages and eventually came away with a packet of small rubbery rags, brightly-coloured, all different shapes and sizes, labelled 24 ASSORTED BALLOONS. He was fascinated by them. He filled them with water and squirted them until everyone got fed up with him, and then he discovered that you could blow into them and make them bigger and bigger. This got him very excited. He blew into a red one until he was quite exhausted, and the rag became a large round red bubble. "Look!" said Stanley, dancing up and down and waving his balloon around, and at that moment there was a loud bang and it wasn't there any more. "Look at what?" said Ned. "You want to watch it with those things. Make a nasty noise."

Stanley examined the piece of torn red stuff in his hand. He threw it down impatiently and picked up another. "Too much blow," he explained. "Have to practise." After a bit he got quite good at it and discovered how to tie the ends up so that the air didn't come out again, and presently he had a whole heap of balloons, round and oblong, red and green and blue and yellow. We were in an open grassy place by a small river, near the middle of the town, and there was quite a strong wind blowing. One of the balloons rose into the air and drifted slowly away. "Bother," said Stanley. He watched the balloon float away over the treetops, getting higher and higher, and a thoughtful look came over his face. "I wonder . . ." he muttered. He went off to the boat and fetched a piece of string from his box of precious things.

I said, "Stanley, what are you playing at?" I always suspect Stanley when he goes very quiet and intent. It can lead to trouble.

"I'm not playing," snapped Stanley. "I'm inventing." He was busy blowing up more balloons and tying them together in a bunch with string. "Can't you *see* . . ." he went on impatiently. We'd all gathered round by now, staring. Pansy patted one of the balloons with her paw and it disappeared with a bang, like the other one. She shot under a bush and Stanley told her furiously to leave it alone. "I'm inventing flying, you stupids," he said. "For animals who haven't got wings. What you do," he explained breathlessly, pausing for a moment between blowing and tying, "what you do is you tie a whole lot of them together—like that—and then you find some sort of seat to sit on . . ." He looked round frantically, caught sight of his old basket, now rather battered, and grabbed hold of it ". . . and you tie *that* on to the end of the string so that it hangs down underneath the balloons—so—and then you . . ."

Pansy, who had come out from under the bush, said, "Can I get in it?"

"I s'pose so," said Stanley, intent on strengthening a knot. "Just till I'm ready. Actually this is the most brilliant idea I've ever had, and in a minute I'm going to show you me flying. Me flying for the second time . . ." He crouched over the basket, tying the string to it more securely. Pansy got into the basket. Above, the balloons were drifting about in the wind, tugging at the basket so that it began to move along the ground a little, and lift up a bit. "Ooh . . ." said Pansy excitedly. "Can I fly too?"

"No," said Stanley. "Wait a minute—better have more string in case it breaks." He turned to go back to the boat again, let go of the string and the basket, and at the very moment he did so there was a sudden strong gust of wind. The balloons went sailing up into the air, and with them the basket, and in the basket Pansy, peering terrified over the edge.

Stanley made a wild leap to catch hold of the string, but

already it was far above our heads, careering away in the wind, the basket wildly swinging beneath. We looked at one another in horror.

"Stanley," said Ned, "how d'you get that thing to stop and come down again?"

Stanley gazed up into the sky at the basket, getting smaller and smaller as the balloons rose higher and higher. We could no longer see Pansy. He said in a small, stunned voice, "I hadn't invented that bit yet."

"Well, you've been and gone and done it then, haven't you?" said Ned. "This time."

Stanley sank down into a huddle. "I'm stupid," he howled, "I'm the most stupid creature that ever was. I'm a nothing. I'm a dreadful mistake. I ought to be got rid of." He was completely distraught.

"Pull yourself together," said Freda sharply. "No good going on like that. What's done's done. How do we get her back again, that's what you've got to think about now, Stanley."

Stanley lay on the ground and moaned. I said, "If those things burst, like the other ones did, the basket will come down."

"It might just go on going up and up," said Ned gloomily. He stared at the sky. The balloons and the basket were now completely out of sight.

Stanley sat up. "I don't think so," he said, "because the air comes out of them slowly, even when you've tied them up. I was trying to invent a way of stopping it but I hadn't got that far yet. So I think," he went on, sounding suddenly hopeful, "I think it'll come down. But it might take quite a long time."

"And it could go a long way before it does," I said. It was an unpromising situation. We looked at each other, and then up at the sky again.

Stanley said, "It's all my fault." He gazed solemnly at

us and went on, "I hereby swear and promise on all my most precious things"—he scrabbled around for his box and his books and his violin—"that I shall find Pansy. Even if I die doing it," he concluded dramatically.

"That's a nice thought, dear," said Freda. "What about London?"

"London can wait," said Stanley grandly.

And thus it was that the voyage of QV 66 was interrupted, through no choice of ours though in the light of at least one thing that happened I suppose it was not altogether a bad thing. And it has to be admitted that it was entirely Stanley's fault—or at least almost entirely. But, as Stanley says when he is in one of his confiding and explaining moods (confiding and explaining about himself, usually), the things that one does are part of the sort of person that one is, and he is never sure if there is anything that can be done about that or not. Sometimes, he says, I think you can make yourself different just by trying, and sometimes I don't. Freda, at this point, usually interrupts and says, oh no, Stanley, I don't think you're right there, dear, I mean people can't help how they're made, can they, I couldn't climb trees like you can, not if I tried for a hundred years, or hold on to things with my tail. And Stanley says loftily, we're not talking about tails, Freda, we're talking about one's Nature. Personally, that kind of talk gets me confused, and one time I find myself agreeing with Stanley and other times with Freda. All I know is, there are one or two things I can't stop myself doing, like chasing rabbits, and never mind tails or Nature or anything else. Perhaps that is what Stanley means.

But all that is not really to the point. What is very much to the point is that because of Stanley's Nature, or whatever you care to call it, we lost Pansy in Oxford and had to abandon the voyage to find her again.

7

*In which the voyage is held up by the hunt for Pansy;
the Major joins the crew of QV 66 and Stanley is
imprisoned in the vaults of Barclays Bank*

We had no idea where to start, at first. And then Offa
pointed out that we must go in the direction of the wind,
because that was where the balloons would have gone.
"Personal experience," he explained. "High wind—very
tricky flying. Takes you with it." And the wind, it seemed,
was blowing towards the south-west. We had to make the
difficult decision as to whether it would be better to
abandon QV 66, at least until we had found Pansy again,
or not. We could get along more quickly without it, if we
were travelling through dry country, but then we would
be stuck if we came to water again. It was hard to know
what lay ahead. Certainly there seemed to be less and less
water all the time. Ned and Freda were both in favour of
abandoning the boat. Stanley was very distressed. "What
about all my things?" he complained, hugging the violin.
"I need them, don't I?" "You didn't need them when you
hadn't got them," said Ned. "You were quite all right
without them then." But we had to promise to come back
for them eventually. Stanley tied QV 66 up to a post beside
the river, very securely, and covered his possessions up

with branches and leaves, and we set off in a south-westerly direction.

Offa flew ahead, making enquiries of other birds that he met, and returning at regular intervals to report. At first things seemed quite promising. Pansy had been sighted quite a number of times, drifting high above the trees, causing considerable consternation among flocks of star-lings, pigeons, rooks and suchlike who wanted to know what the world was coming to when, apparently, cats could fly. Offa explained that the circumstances were exceptional, and then they were prepared to be cooperative and give information about when she had been seen, and where, and so forth. For the rest of that day, hurrying as fast as we could across country, we followed Offa.

By the evening we had climbed a range of hills, and when it got too dark to travel any more we settled down for the night. But, as we were uncomfortably aware, the wind does not necessarily drop at night. Pansy would be flying on ahead, getting farther and farther away all the time. We slept badly, thinking of this.

During the next few days we found that, as we had feared, news of Pansy became more scarce. Offa continued to enquire ahead, and the answers got vaguer and vaguer. Yes, someone would say, they remembered seeing some-thing very odd in the sky that wasn't a bird or a cloud, but they couldn't think now exactly when it had been: the day before yesterday, several days ago, long ago . . . Birds are never very definite about time; they only know about nesting or not nesting, migrating or not migrating. You can never have a satisfactory conversation with a bird; they are always repeating things they have heard from someone else, and haven't a personal opinion between them. Offa, of course, is something of an exception, having had an unusual upbringing, but as you may have gathered, even he can go on in a somewhat tedious manner when the mood takes him. Stanley, who finds birds exasperating, became quite enraged with the vagueness of a group of lapwings from whom we were trying to get information. "Woolly-headed lot!" he fumed. "What do you mean—you don't really *know*? Either you saw it or you didn't!" The lapwings flew off, with loud depressing cries. We decided that, in the absence of firm news, the best thing we could do was to push on in the same direction and hope for the best.

We travelled for many days. Every now and then we would come across some bird or animal who remembered seeing Pansy and the basket. Stanley was certain that the balloons would not have lasted very long—a few days at most—so that what we had to do was try to trace the way they had gone, and hope to come across someone who remembered seeing them come down to earth, or who had seen Pansy since. It was fortunate that she was so distinctive. There are not that many cats with bright orange patches around. Offa did a great deal of enquiring, flying here, there and everywhere, while we plodded on at ground level. Sometimes he would come back with news of a sighting in some quite different direction, so that we had to switch to left or right, or even retrace our steps. We didn't come across anyone who had seen the basket come down to earth.

It meant, of course, that we were more in touch with other animals and birds than usual. I don't mean that we had been stand-offish before, or kept ourselves to ourselves or anything like that; it's just that when you are on the move all the time you don't get that much opportunity to make contact with others, except to pass the time of day and that kind of thing. Now, we were always chatting to cows, horses, rabbits, dogs, cats—whoever we happened

97

to come across. They weren't always that willing to talk. They'd stare at us, sometimes (nothing unusual about that, given Stanley's presence) and then find they had some urgent business elsewhere and move off before we had time for a proper talk. Ned said, one day, "Bit unforthcoming, aren't they—folk round here?"

Freda agreed. "Animals used to be ever so much more friendly."

It was true; I'd been noticing just the same thing. We hadn't come across any other instances of really lunatic behaviour, like those packs of dogs in Manchester. It was just that everyone seemed concerned to keep themselves apart, like with like as it were, so that you seldom saw sheep grazing with cows, say, and there seemed to be a good deal of unnecessary aggression. Everyone thought we were completely mad—in the first place for associating with one another, in the second for travelling around in this way, and for being so worried about Pansy. "So she got lost?" said a mangy black tomcat, sitting on a gatepost. "So what? So you forget about her."

"She was our *friend*," snapped Stanley.

"So you find another," yawned the tom. "There's always company to be had for the asking."

Stanley said in withering tones, "One gets attached to people, as it happens."

"Oh, I don't know," said the tom. "Easy come, easy go—that's my philosophy."

Stanley turned his back on him and walked off in disgust. Later he became very excited and emotional about friends and the importance thereof, which annoyed Ned. "O.K., O.K., mate," he said. "True enough and all that. But one doesn't *talk* about it."

Stanley accused him of not having any feelings. "On the contrary," said Ned with dignity, "one experiences a good deal of heave and stir, as it happens. One just doesn't make a meal of it. Unlike some."

He and Stanley glared at each other; if you hadn't known you would not have taken them for friends at all. I changed the subject, hastily.

It was not long after this that Offa came back from one of his flights in search of information much offended by the behaviour of a crowd of rooks who were, apparently, tormenting some other bird. "Shocking," he panted in agitation. "Disgraceful. Going on about pecking its eyes out, finishing it off . . . Horrible business."

Freda tutted. "What was it?"

"Couldn't quite see," said Offa. "Bright red, that's all I can tell you."

I said there are no such things as bright red birds.

"This one was," said Offa. "It was like nothing you ever saw. Peculiar."

Stanley, who had been fiddling with some sticks and bits of metal, trying to make himself a tool (he still mourned his box of precious things) pricked up his ears. "Like me?"

"Like you only a bird," said Offa. "Come on. Ought to do something about it. Can't have that kind of thing going on." He flew off, with the rest of us following.

The rooks were swirling around a small tree, cawing excitely and egging each other on. Every now and then one of them would swoop at the tree and strike out with beak and claws at something cowering on a branch. It was a thoroughly disagreeable spectacle. I barked at them to clear off, and they croaked back rude remarks about interfering so-and-so's who should mind their own business. They even made some aggressive swoops at us until Stanley began to hurl stones at them. We could see the bird now, about Offa's size, and, just as he had said, bright scarlet, crouched miserably behind a screen of

leaves. The rooks, retreating from Stanley's volley of stones, lifted away from the tree, screaming abuse, and finally flew off with a great deal of threatening and unsavoury language. We gathered round the tree and stared at the bird, which was indeed quite extraordinary. It was bright red with a grey tail, curved and scaly feet with which it clung to the branch, and a huge curved beak and bright black eyes over which dropped, from time to time, as if in a long slow wink, grey and wrinkled eyelids.

"Well, I never!" whispered Freda. "Foreign-looking, I call that, but I suppose it can't help it, poor thing."

"Morning," said Ned. "Everything all right, mate?"

The bird drooped one eyelid wearily and then cocked its head sideways to look at us. "AttenSHUN!" it croaked. "Stand-at-EASE! Please be upstanding for the loyal toast. Mine's a small scotch, colonel."

"Pardon?" said Ned.

With a lurch, the bird toppled suddenly from its branch and fluttered awkwardly to the ground. We saw now that it was in a very mangy state, its feathers battered and in some places missing altogether; it was hardly able to fly at all. It huddled on the ground and said mournfully, "Not quite up to the mark these days, I'm afraid. Bit under the weather. Thought it was all up just then—very grateful to you."

Stanley, who was deeply interested, edged closer. "What are you?" he said.

"Major Trumpington-Smith," said the bird. He scratched his head with one claw, lurched sideways and said bravely, "Chin up! Stiff upper lip! Honour of the regiment and all that." And then he collapsed altogether, eyes closed—a bedraggled heap of scarlet and grey feathers piled amid the leafmould. "Poor thing," said Freda. "You can see he's had a bad time."

The bird recovered gradually. Stanley found him some nuts, to which he was apparently especially partial, and as he ate—he seemed to be half-starved—he began to perk up and told us how he had been chivvied from one place to another by tormenting flocks of starlings or rooks as he became weaker and weaker and less able to fly. Not, he explained, that he had ever been a particularly strong flyer, never, apparently, having done much of it, for reasons which were vague. Indeed his entire background remained extremely unclear. When pressed about where he came from, and if there were others like him there, he chattered on in a confused fashion about places he referred to as the Barracks, and the Mess, and the Parade Ground and Battalion H.Q. He said he was extremely old. Stanley, who thinks he is about four, kept questioning him about this, but the bird became more and more imprecise. He said he thought he was about a hundred and eighty, or on the other hand it might be three hundred and six, he'd never been awfully good at that sort of thing. But what did emerge from his rather bewildering account of himself, or at least what seemed to—was that at some point in his past he had lived with People.

"People!" said Freda, horrified. "How awful!"

"Not at all," said the bird. "Awfully decent set of chaps. Fine body of men. Guards regiment, of course." He cracked a nut in his powerful beak and went on sadly, "Don't know what happened to 'em all. Haven't seen 'em for a long time." He had been, it seemed, very well looked after by the People and gave us vague and incoherent accounts of being carried on a perch while People walked up and down in lines and something called a band played music very loudly.

"Music?" said Stanley. "I've just been inventing that, before I had to leave my violin behind. What sort of music?"

The bird put the nut down and whistled a bouncy tune. Ned jigged up and down appreciatively. "I like that," he said. "Very nice. Got a bit of go to it. Not like that fancy stuff of yours, Stanley." Stanley looked contemptuous and muttered something about mediocre and commonplace. But he was still much interested in the bird, and obviously didn't want to offend him. He kept on asking him more and more questions: about what he could remember and what had happened to him and so forth. And what he was. The bird was vague about a good many things, but he did come up with a few pieces of hard information. He was a parrot, apparently ("Trumpington-Smith by name—just call me Major"), and no, he couldn't remember ever having come across anyone else like Stanley, and no, he had no idea when the People went, or where to, or why. One day they'd been there and then somehow they weren't, and there was water everywhere.

Stanley, after hearing that the Major was also without friends or relations, became very intimate and confidential; clearly he felt he'd found a soul-mate at last. The Major, though, was not entirely sympathetic. Not knowing, or never having known, any other parrots, didn't seem to bother him in the least. The mention of London, on the other hand, got him quite excited. He had been there, in the dim distant past, and talked nostalgically of Trooping the Colour and Horseguards Parade and Buckingham Palace. "What was it *like*?" said Stanley impatiently. "Are you *sure* you didn't see anyone like me?" The Major shook his head. "Kensington Barracks . . ." he said dreamily. "The Mall . . . Those were the days. Love to have another look at the old place."

"Come along with us, then," said Ned airily, and that, to cut a long story short, is how the Major joined the crew of QV 66, although at the time, of course, QV 66 was tied up to a bridge at Oxford, miles and miles away. He was really a very agreeable bird, despite a rather irritating habit of squawking orders at people when over-excited, which we soon learned to ignore, and a tendency to whistle which maddened Stanley. "Do you mind?" he'd moan. "One does just happen to be rather sensitive." "All right, old chap, all right," the Major would say amiably, "just trying to jolly things along a bit, that's all."

Now that he was with us, and no longer persecuted by other birds as he had been for so long, the Major picked up rapidly, grew new feathers and even recovered his flying powers, though he was never all that enthusiastic about flying and preferred to travel perched on the back of either Ned or Freda, whistling when Stanley was out of earshot. We all became very attached to him, though there was sometimes a certain amount of rivalry between him and Stanley: they did not really have all that much in common apart from being unique of their kind. The Major also turned out to be a storyteller, which made Stanley jealous. He told confused and exaggerated stories which we did not entirely believe about campaigns and battles and "shows" of one kind and another in which he claimed he had been involved. He would ramble on about Omdurman and Ladysmith and the Khyber Pass and Stanley would sit a little way away, pretending not to listen and making contemptuous noises from time to time. Then Stanley would embark on one of his own most grandiose and elaborate tales about kings and queens and heroes, in order to keep his end up. Between the two of them we had no shortage of entertainment.

Don't imagine, though, that we had forgotten about Pansy. Not a bit of it. The Major, when he had been told the story of her disappearance, became as keen as the rest of us to find her again. "Always glad to help a lady in distress," he explained. He had, as Freda was always pointing out, very nice manners. "Old-fashioned," said Freda with approval, "not like some people I could mention." She stared pointedly at Stanley, who stared back and pulled a face at her as soon as she wasn't looking.

We were in hilly country; not the steep craggy hills that we had known when we first began the voyage but wide rolling grassy hills where a great many sheep and cattle grazed and there were few towns but many villages scattered in the valleys. Once or twice we came to larger places—Newbury, Andover—and skirted them, keeping to the country and enquiring about Pansy all the time. Once, our hopes were raised by a party of rabbits who said they remembered a day not all that long ago when a strange object had come down out of the sky over thataway and yes, as far as they knew it was still there. So, in great excitement, we trekked several miles to the east and found, eventually, their strange object, which was nothing but one of the People's umbrellas, lodged in a bramble-bush. We turned south again.

On another occasion some starlings chattered away about a peculiar orange creature—a cat maybe—living in a ruined house nearby, but when at last we found it, it turned out to be nothing but a large and very bad-tempered stoat. Stanley, who had gone into the house to investigate, came out in a hurry, nursing a bitten hand and complaining about animals who wouldn't answer a perfectly simple question. We calmed him down and went on our way.

Not long after that we reached a small town where we stopped to rest for a few days, partly because Freda had lamed herself and needed to recover, and partly because there was a shop there with a storeroom full of sacks of nuts, which were too much for Stanley and the Major to resist; the one thing they do share is a passion for nuts.

105

So Freda had a peaceful time grazing on the grassy place in the middle of the town, Stanley and the Major gorged themselves on walnuts, brazils and hazelnuts, and the rest of us wandered around and enjoyed a spell of hot weather which had followed a long period of rain. The little town was much like any other—the buildings mostly half-ruined, but with interesting scavengings to be had in one way or another, the streets cracked and overgown with weeds, the odd sheep or bullock strolling around in search of windfall apples or other pickings. Stanley, as usual, went dashing in and out of houses and shops, reappearing with various treasures he had found by way of tools, books, pencils and one thing and another.

He was particularly fascinated by one place with a gold-lettered sign outside saying Barclays Bank, and came out with handfuls of round metal things, silver and brown, each of them with writing on and a picture of a Person. He arranged them in rows on the street outside and invented an elaborate game which he played with the Major, all to do with squares that he drew with one of his pencils, and two armies of the round things, his side and the Major's side. I never could follow what the rules of the game were, but it gave rise to a great deal of argument and ill feeling because Stanley kept losing and eventually flounced off in a temper. He went back into Barclays Bank and we could hear him banging about inside, throwing things around and grumbling. As you may have gathered, Stanley is not at all good at controlling his feelings.

Presently there was silence, and we forgot about him— or at least so far as you ever can forget about Stanley. I was dozing in the sun and the Major was telling a long boring story about something called the Relief of Mafeking. Offa was sitting on some iron railing, preening himself. The others were somewhere around. Presently we all became conscious of a faint, distant shouting. "Help!" it seemed to be saying. "Oh, help!"

"A voice crying in the wilderness," said Offa comfortably, turning his attention to the other wing. The Major, who was in the middle of a complicated account of muskets and holding your fire and outflanking movements, cocked his head on one side for a moment, and then went on with what he was saying. Freda came ambling over and said, "Where's Stanley?"

And then it dawned on us what the shouting was. "Trouble," said Ned wearily. "Here we go again. Hold on, young Stanley, be with you in a moment." We trooped into the bank; the shouting was coming from somewhere in there.

At first there was nothing to be seen. There was a mass of rubble inside, the remains of the roof which had fallen in, and a few saplings poking up through it, and a lot of rubbish scattered around and large paper bags, some of them still full of the metal things that Stanley and the Major had been playing their game with. And then we spotted a staircase in one corner, going down, apparently to some cellars. It was partly choked with bricks and rubble, but we could just squeeze down it, even Ned and Freda; it was from down there that Stanley was shouting.

At the bottom of the stairs there was a huge heavy door, half-open, with a sign on it saying Strongroom. Ned heaved it open with his shoulder and we found ourselves in a big gloomy room, almost dark except for a glimmer through a dirty skylight in one corner. There were metal cupboards all over one wall, and at the other side was a massive arrangement of steel bars and wire mesh, completely shutting off one end of the room like a large cage. There was a wire mesh door in the cage, firmly closed, and inside the cage were bags upon bags from which spilled bundles of what appeared to be oblong pieces of paper. There were a great many of the metal things, too, strewn about the floor.

In the middle of them, gazing out at us through the steel bar and the wire mesh, sat Stanley, saying feebly, "Help!"

8

In which the Major organises Operation Airhole, and the animals find themselves at Stonehenge in time for a thunderstorm and a good deal else besides

Freda said, "Stanley, you come out of there this minute!"

"I can't," said Stanley.

"What do you mean—you can't?"

Stanley's eyes filled with tears. His voice quavered. "I was fiddling with the lock, to see how it works, and now it won't open any more." He rattled the door, to demonstrate.

"Now you've been and gone and done it, haven't you?" said Ned crossly.

Stanley rolled himself up into a ball and moaned. "I'm going to be shut up here for ever and ever and die."

"Very bad show," agreed the Major. "Most unfortunate."

I told Stanley to pull himself together and not be silly— of course we weren't going to leave him there. We'd get him out somehow. Truth to tell, though, I couldn't see how. The steel bars of the cage were quite unbreakable, and the wire mesh too thick and strong to cut with any tool that Stanley could use, even if we could find one. The Major was swarming up and down it, trying to wrench a hole with his powerful beak, unsuccessfully. The lock that

Stanley had been fiddling with had a keyhole, but no key, of course.

"I'm hungry," said Stanley.

For the rest of the day we searched for keys, and found one or two but none that would fit. The Major found a rusty saw and we managed to pass it to Stanley under the door, but he could make no impression on the strong mesh. He sat there eating a great many nuts (to keep his strength up, he said) and complaining that he was cold. The Major, perched on a pile of bricks, said that seeing Stanley sitting there in a cage like that reminded him of something. Stanley's small hairy hand came poking through the mesh at regular intervals, demanding more nuts and the Major scratched his head and said it was a funny thing, and he couldn't for the life of him tell you when or where, but he had a feeling he'd seen this before, somewhere . . . "Never mind about that," said Stanley impatiently. "*Do* something. Get me out of here."

We tried everything we could think of. We scraped and hammered at the mesh, and Ned hurled his whole weight at it, time and again, and only succeeded in making himself sore. Finally, as night fell, we settled down gloomily in the cellar, Stanley having pleaded with us not to leave him alone in the dark. He was very miserable, and feeling slightly ill from having eaten too many nuts.

In the morning Freda complained that she had a stiff neck. There'd been the most terrible draught, she said, all night, howling down on her. Now she was as stiff as a poker—she moved her head from side to side, awkwardly, to demonstrate. "At least you're not in a prison," said Stanley, in his most pathetic voice. "I wish *I* had nothing to worry about but a stiff neck." Everybody was irritable and snappy. Freda said she'd go mad with claustrophobia if she had to stay down here much longer and Offa kept

110

droning on about the dark places of the earth and the uttermost pits of hell and Stanley became very grand and martyred and said we'd better all go away and leave him to die slowly of starvation, he didn't care, and it wouldn't be his fault if we felt sorry about it for the rest of our lives. I sat there feeling fed up with them all. I wondered if I could possibly dig a hole through the stone floor and get get Stanley out that way, and knew that I couldn't.

"Draught?" said the Major pensively, staring up at the ceiling, his head cocked on one side. "Cold air? Where from?"

"There," said Freda, "that square thing up there."

In the middle of the ceiling of Stanley's cage there was a small square hole covered with fine rusty wire mesh. We had none of us noticed it before. Now, we all gazed upwards.

"Stanley, my boy," said the Major, "could you get up there?" Stanley said he thought he probably could. He climbed up the inside of the wire at the front of the cage and then found that if he reached out he could just catch hold of a torn corner of the wire netting over the hole. He swung from it for a moment and then dropped down on to the floor again.

The Major said busily, "Right! Operation Airhole. Reconnaissance party proceed outside at the double."

"Come again?" said Ned, but the Major had already hurried off up the stairs, squawking orders at himself and anyone else who cared to listen.

We all went after him. Outside, we saw the Major's small scarlet person clambering awkwardly over the rubble and weeds around the bank, saying, "Here we go then . . . Oops-a-daisy . . . No, we don't . . . Just let's have a peep in here . . . No go . . . Pause and reconsider strategy . . . Over the top, men . . . Report back to base." I joined him

111

and began sniffing around and presently I found a place where amongst a muddle of smells I could detect a faint but unmistakable whiff of Stanley. I pointed this out to the Major, and between us we scrabbled away and uncovered the opening of a narrow pipe. The Major cocked his head on one side and peered down into it. Then he whistled. From somewhere below there was a distant cry. The Major nodded. "Got it!" he said. "Good work, chaps. Better press on, then." And with that he disappeared down the hole. It was just wide enough for him.

The rest of us went back into the cellar again. Stanley was fidgeting about in excitement, staring up at the airhole. "Stanley," said Ned, "you are about to be rescued, by my reckoning. And mind you be properly grateful."

"I do hope the Major's all right," said Freda anxiously. "I do think he was ever so brave to go down that nasty dark hole."

After what seemed an age there was a scrabbling sound on the other side of the wire-netting, and a flash of scarlet. "Objective achieved," said the Major's voice, and a scaly claw reached round the torn bit of netting. "Operation wire-cutting," he went on breathlessly. "Stand by to evacuate, young Stanley." There was a great deal of wrenching and tearing of the wire by the Major's claws and strong beak, and after a minute or so he had it all ripped away and his head and beady eye peered out of the hole. "Upsy-daisy, now," he said to Stanley, and Stanley went swarming up the cage-front and across to the hole. The Major backed away and we saw Stanley's head disappear, and then the rest of him, so that only his tail hung out. We heard his muffled voice say "Help! Tight! Stuck!", and the Major making noises of encouragement and exhortation, and then slowly, inch by inch, the rest of Stanley vanished into the hole. There were squeakings and gaspings that became gradually more indistinct, and we all went outside and waited at the exit to the airhole.

Half an hour later the Major emerged, followed by a very dusty and battered Stanley who collapsed on to the ground.

"Bit of difficulty here and there," explained the Major, with a glance at Stanley. "Too fat."

"I told you not to eat so many nuts," said Freda. "Now say thank you nicely."

Stanley, though, was too breathless to say anything at all. He lay flat on his back panting and groaning. After a bit he sat up and said, "Am I still the same shape?"

"More's the pity," said Ned unkindly. "Bit of luck and you might have ended up looking like an ordinary straightforward animal."

Stanley gave him a withering look and said, "Actually I was very clever in that hole because I made myself long and thin like a snake, so that I could get through. I expect I could do it again if I tried." He stretched out one leg and wriggled it experimentally. "Animals like me can do that," he said. "It's very useful. Actually if we want to we can change into something quite different."

"Go on then," said Freda. "Let's see."

"Some other time," said Stanley. "I'm hungry now. What happened to the rest of those nuts?"

Even Stanley had to admit—grudgingly—that the Major was the hero of the hour. He sat rearranging his ruffled feathers and saying modestly that he'd had a bit of luck, that was all. "Never been a brainy chap. Just a matter of plodding away at things. It's organisation that counts." Stanley cracked nuts, with an unnecessary amount of noise, and looked supercilious.

We left the village and moved on, across huge downland fields where a great many sheep were grazing. None of them would admit to having seen Pansy, but sheep are always hopeless about information. They all have to ask each other about everything and then eventually come up with something vague and noncommittal that is no help at all. However, at the end of a couple of days Offa, who had been doing his usual prospective flying around, came back with some news that sounded definitely promising. He had met a flock of wood pigeons who remembered seeing a brightly coloured cat not long before, at a place a few miles to the west. "Rejoice with me, for I have found my sheep which was lost. She was lost and is found. Hosanna, for our salvation is come . . ."

We told him to shut up and tell us which way to go.

The curious thing was that everyone seemed to be going in that direction. It didn't strike us for quite a while, and

114

then the Major, who had been travelling in his favourite position on Ned's back, with his claws comfortably dug into Ned's brown mane, said, "Bit of a rum do, eh? General movement of things . . ." I looked round—we were going along the ridge of a hill, with views around into the valleys at either side—and saw what he meant. Everywhere there were little groups of animals, all going west, like us: small gatherings of sheep, a huddle of bullocks, a few cows, solitary foxes sloping along beside a hedge, dogs trotting across a field, and flocks of birds overhead—rooks, starlings, lapwings, an isolated kestrel. Nothing hurried, but everything was purposeful: a slow, determined movement towards the setting sun, which hung large and low in the sky ahead of us. It was almost midsummer, and the days were long.

"That's funny," said Stanley.

"I expect there's some nice grass there," said Freda. "That's why everyone wants to go that way."

We caught up with a gaggle of bullocks, and asked them where they were going. "To the Place, of course," they snorted. "What d'yer think? Stupid question . . ."

"What Place?" I asked, patiently, and they all rolled their eyes around and made remarks about the ignorance of some people.

I ploughed on doggedly (if you'll pardon the expression) and said, "Why all go there at once?"

"Got to, haven't you?" said the bullocks. "It's the Time, isn't it? Got to go the Place at the Time, every year. Stands to reason, doesn't it?"

I gave up.

There was not much more information to be got from anything else, either. Offa waylaid some collared doves, resting in a tree, but they just burbled on about the sun, and having to get there before it began. Sheep weren't

115

even worth bothering with. An elderly collie seemed more promising at first, but then he blathered on with a long rigmarole about how one had always gone there then, ever since he could remember, and it might be dangerous not to so one went on doing it, and in any case everyone else did, didn't they?

"What *for*?" said Stanley, at which the collie just stared at us in surprise and said that everybody must, mustn't they? in case it didn't happen.

"In case *what* didn't happen?"

But the collie had already padded off, muttering about crazy foreigners who didn't know anything about anything.

We could get no more news of Pansy, either. All the animals were either too preoccupied with the movement west, or too vague, or too unwilling to talk. The place to which the wood pigeons had referred was called Durrington and as far as we could make out we were not too far away from it, just a matter of a few miles. We spent the night—a wet, dismal one—in the shelter of a hedge, with a field of travelling sheep on the other side of it. They kept us awake half the night bleating on about the end of the world or something. We didn't pay much attention to them, or we might have been better prepared for what was to come.

In the morning the rain-clouds had rolled away and there was a bright, warm sun. The sheep seemed more cheerful, and moved off early. We followed them at a distance, climbing slowly up a wide, rolling hill, which was flecked in all directions with moving animals. When we got to the top of it we could see that the whole landscape was the same; as far as you could see, for mile upon mile, there were little droves of travelling creatures. The sky was busy with birds.

I jumped on to the top of a low stone wall, and stood

there looking around. I felt uneasy. Twitchy. There was a sense of something being about to happen, and you could not know what on earth it might be. The air was heavy and thundery: I could smell rain. The others, too, were affected by the atmosphere. Freda was edgy and nervous, and Ned kept prancing about and neighing. Only Stanley was unperturbed. "Come on, you lot," he said. "What's the matter?" Offa, who had been circling around overhead, dropped down and said, "And there was a vast multitude of creatures gathered, all manner of creation, the fowls of the air and the fishes of the sea. I've seen this Place they're talking about. Lot of enormous stones stuck up on their ends in the middle of nowhere, in a circle. Most unusual."

"A house?" I asked.

Offa shook his head. "Not a house. Makes you think of churches, somehow, but it's not one of those either. No roof."

"Something the People built?"

"Must've been," said Offa. "I'll tell you one thing, though," he went on solemnly, "I've never come across anything like it, and that's for sure."

All day we travelled through wide fields and along tracks over the hills. And then, as the sun was beginning to go down, we came to the top of a ridge and saw it, in the distance, just as Offa had said—great grey blocks of stone standing in a circle, dark against the flaming orange sky. All around there was a vast crowd of animals. Even Stanley was impressed. We stayed there in silence, the six of us, staring, while other creatures streamed steadily past towards the stones, following a track with one of the People's signs on it that said STONEHENGE $2\frac{1}{4}$.

"I don't like it," said Freda uneasily. "It gives me the creeps, somehow. What's it for?"

"It's for playing a game," said Stanley, without quite

117

his usual confidence. "You chase each other in and out of the stones, you see, and the one who gets round quickest . . ." His voice trailed away. "No," he said, "it's not. It's been a kind of enormous house, only the roof fell in."

"Defensive position?" offered the Major. "Withdrawal of troops in face of approaching enemy?" But he didn't sound very certain either.

And then, as we watched, the sun sank down behind the stones until there was just a scarlet rim resting above them, and as it did so there came what sounded like a great wailing and moaning from all the animals. The landscape hummed with it. And at the same moment there was a roll of thunder from somewhere far away, growing louder and nearer. Freda mooed nervously. "Nasty bit of weather coming up," said Ned, in an uncomfortable voice. We none of us like storms.

By the time we got close to the stones the sun had sunk below the horizon and dark rain-clouds hung overhead. The first drops began to fall, warm and heavy, as we reached the outer ring of stones, winding our way through the groups of animals. Stanley was scampering on ahead to get a closer look when all of a sudden we saw a dark shape swoop down and hover threateningly above him. It was a great black crow. "That'll do," it croaked. "Keep off. Officials only in the Place."

And now, for the first time, we noticed the crows. There were dozens of them, it seemed, perched all over the stones like sinister shadows, hunched shapes staring out at the darkening countryside and the gathered animals.

"Nonsense," said Stanley, annoyed. He had stopped, though; the crow had a huge stabbing bill. It swooped to and fro above his head. Some of the others shuffled along the nearest stone, getting closer. Behind me, a voice said softly, "I should tell your friend to watch out. They can get nasty."

118

I looked round. The speaker was a sheepdog, sitting on his haunches a few yards away. "Take my advice," he went on, out of the side of his mouth. "I know. I've seen 'em when they take a dislike to someone."

I said, "Stanley . . ."

Stanley was getting into a temper. He chattered at the crow indignantly. "I've got just as much right here as you have."

"No need for any unpleasantness," said Freda. "Now, Stanley, I'm sure everything can be sorted out nicely."

"Out!" said the crow. "Clear off!"

"I don't see why . . ." Stanley began. He took a few steps forwards, and the crow lunged at him. Several others lifted from where they were perched and dived down towards him. Stanley screamed and shot backwards; there was blood on his fur.

We retreated to a nearby ditch. "Very ungentlemanly behaviour," said the Major. "Not our kind of chaps at all. Any first aid needed?"

Stanley sat staring balefully at the crows. He wasn't very badly hurt. "It could have *damaged* me," he said. "It could have *killed* me."

"Dead right, son," agreed Ned.

I said to the sheepdog, who had joined us in the ditch, "Who are they?"

"The Wise Ones," said the sheepdog. "What neck of the woods do you people come from, not knowing that?"

I said we'd been travelling a long time. Stanley said he'd like to know just what it was they were so wise about. The sheepdog gave him a warning glance and said it might be as well to keep one's voice down.

He seemed friendly enough—the first reasonably agreeable animal we'd come across for some time, indeed. I decided to make a friend of him, and told him about our journey, and the reasons for it, and the search for Pansy.

119

When I mentioned her, he looked disturbed for a moment. I asked if he'd seen her. "'Fraid not," he said. "Just it occurred to me that possibly . . . Let's hope not, anyway. Carry on."

I said that that was about it, and asked him to explain what precisely was going on. The others gathered round to listen.

"Seems funny," said the sheepdog, "having to *tell* anyone . . . but seeing as how you're strangers. It's the ceremony tomorrow, you see. The ceremony we have to have at the Place every year. The Wise Ones do it. They're the only ones who know how to. Mind you," he went on, looking away with what seemed to be embarrassment, "a lot of us aren't all that keen on it. We don't like the—well, the ceremony bit. But it's got to be done, too much of a risk not to, if you didn't it mightn't . . ." He shrugged, awkwardly. "Well, it just mightn't ever come up again."

"What mightn't come up?" said Stanley.

"The sun, of course."

We all stared at the sheepdog in astonishment.

"Hold it a minute," said Ned. "Just to get this right. You have some kind of ceremony here, tomorrow, to make sure the sun comes up again?"

The sheepdog nodded solemnly.

"But it always does, doesn't it?" said Ned in perplexity. "So why bother?"

Stanley said, "They're mad. Raving mad. Absolutely idiotic."

It was dusk. A deep, thick dusk with rain falling and that thunder lurking still beyond the horizon. I said, "Why tomorrow, particularly?"

"It's the Time, isn't it?" said the sheepdog. "Midsummer. Have to make sure things are going to go on."

Stanley spluttered rudely. The whole conversation was

exasperating him. "Things just do go on," he said, "and that's all there is to it. Having stupid ceremonies isn't going to make any difference to anything."

Freda gave him a look and told him to mind his manners.

"What is this ceremony, then?" said Ned.

The sheepdog looked embarrassed again, and muttered something about the Wise Ones insisting. "Think it's unnecessary, personally," he said.

I said uneasily, "Think what's unnecessary?"

The sheepdog didn't answer for a moment. Then he said, "Killing something."

"Killing an *animal*?" said Freda, appalled. He nodded.

We sat in a shocked silence. "Very bad show indeed," said the Major at last. "Don't care for that at all. Barbaric, what?"

"The Wise Ones say," said the sheepdog, "that the sun must have an offering, or it will be angry and never rise again."

"That sort of thing's all right in stories," said Stanley. "Outside them it's phooey. Phooey and rubbish and stuff and nonsense."

The sheepdog, who was getting more and more uncomfortable, said that quite a lot of them felt like that nowadays, but you couldn't be sure, could you? If you *didn't* do it, you were taking a big risk.

"What animal?" said Freda.

The sheepdog said that it was usually something that nobody wanted. Something a bit peculiar. He glanced at Stanley.

"Oh no they won't," said Stanley.

"It's all right," said the sheepdog. "They've already got it, actually. The starlings said."

"What is it?"

He shook his head. "Don't know. They keep it in the

121

middle of the Place until the Time. We'll find out then. Just before dawn. Better get some kip."

We none of us slept much. The rain stopped after a while but the air was heavy and thick. All around us there were the shiftings and murmurings of the crowds of creatures; there was a sense of waiting. Watching and waiting. Freda said she had a headache. The Major muttered to himself. Offa dozed and woke and rambled on about the temples of the ungodly and graven images and burnt offerings. Stanley sat staring into the darkness. Occasionally he said, "*Stupids*," or, "Wise Ones, huh . . ."

9

In which Stanley is very brave, Pansy is found, an old friend appears out of the blue, and the voyage is resumed

Long before dawn the whole place was awake and moving. There was a faint yellow glimmer in the sky and the animals were all looking towards it from time to time and murmuring among themselves. Flocks of birds flew about chattering. Only the crows sat silent, like black sentinels among the great stones, occasionally croaking or flapping from one perch to another. It was very still and thundery. The sheepdog said that it would not be long now.

We all had this feeling that we must stay, though each of us, I think, would have preferred to go. The atmosphere was intense, brooding and unpleasant. Freda, staring at the sky, said, "Do you think it will?"

"Will what?" I said.

"Rise. The sun."

Stanley gave a howl of rage. "Don't you start going on like that too."

"You never know," said Freda uncomfortably. "S'pose they're right."

"They're not right," said Stanley through clenched teeth. Freda looked at him, and then back to the pale, streaked sky.

The animals were gathering around the stones. For as far as you could see the downland around was covered with them, small restless shapes in the grey light of dawn. We moved to a bit of higher ground where we had a fairly good view of the stone circle, though it was impossible to see clearly into the central area. The crows were even more thickly massed than on the previous evening; they clustered like black fruit and the air was filled with their harsh voices. And then, as we watched, one of them, a huge creature who seemed a size larger than the rest, lifted from the ground and flapped up on to one of the highest stones. A hush fell, and he began to speak: a monotonous, incomprehensible chanting.

I said to the sheepdog, "What's he saying?"

The sheepdog shook his head. "Nobody knows. It's very important, though. The ceremony doesn't work without it."

Stanley was hunched into a ball, his black eyes glaring out, contempt written all over his small wrinkled face.

"Then what?" he said.

"Then—well, then they do the other bit of the ceremony and then we all kind of sing, ask the sun to come up, you know, and after that it does. At least up to now it always has. Then we go away till next year."

"Mad," said Stanley loudly. "Stark, raving mad."

Offa, who was perched on a branch above our heads, had become very alert, shifting up and down and staring at the stone circle. "Hosanna!" he said suddenly. "Excuse me a moment, just thought for a second I saw ... Hope I'm wrong. Back in a minute." He flew up and we saw him make a wide sweep round; some of the crows squinted at him and made threatening noises. He dropped down on to the tree again. I said, "What's wrong?"

"I've seen it," he said. "The animal. The one they—do the next part of the ceremony with. It's Pansy."

124

After a moment I said stupidly, "Are you sure?"

"Quite sure," said Offa. "They've got her in a sort of cage thing, in the middle of the stone circle. They're all sitting round her, chanting. Nasty."

We were silent for another moment or two. Then Freda began pawing the ground with her front feet, and swinging her head from side to side; she only does that when she's about to get in a furious temper. Stanley was swearing, very quietly and steadily. The Major was shuffling from side to side on Ned's back. Ned was snorting.

I said, "Right. What we do is . . ." And then I stopped. I couldn't think, at all, what to do. There were animals on all sides, animals who believed that this idiotic ceremony had to go on; in front, in and all around the stone circle, between us and Pansy, were those evil hordes of crows. I hesitated, trying to think.

It had been getting darker and darker, as though the dawn were going into reverse. There was a searing flash of lightning right overhead, and then almost immediately an ear-splitting crack of thunder. A great moan went up from the encircling animals. The Major was muttering something in my ear about an advance under cover of darkness. Sheep, cows and bullocks were milling about in a confused way, startled by the thunder; it was impossible any longer to hear the droning of the chief crow. The crows themselves seemed to be in a state of some agitation, calling to one another and croaking to the animals to stay still and be quiet or the ceremony could not proceed. There was another flash of lightning, during which I just had time to see that Stanley was no longer beside me. I said "Stanley?", and looked round, but all was black again, and a bunch of pigs went skittering nervously by, barging into us and vanishing into the darkness.

And then, above all the other noises, there came a weird banshee wailing, like nothing I've ever heard before.

"Wurra-wurra-wurra-", it went. "Whee . . . Whee . . .", and trailed away into a blood-curdling howl. It seemed to come from every side—first it was near, and then over there somewhere, and then in quite another direction altogether. It threw the animals into an even greater state of panic; a herd of bullocks came stampeding through the middle of us yelling to each other that this was the end of the world. Birds were flying to and fro calling and twittering.

There was another flash of lightning. It froze the whole scene in a moment's brilliance, brighter than the brightest day: the milling animals, the still cold landscape, the stone circle, the crows. And it gave us all time to see, for a split second, a small dark shape bounding from one stone to another, dodging the crows, leaping and swarming, howling as it went.

Stanley.

Everything went dark again. "Forward," said the Major. "Support force advance at the double . . ."

We pushed our way through the crowd, keeping in touch with one another by shouting. There was such a noise and commotion now that it would be hard for anyone to keep track of us, and in any case everyone else was in too much of a state to take much notice. I could hear the crows flapping about and telling each other to keep on with the ceremony. They were saying something about a devil, too. "Get it!" they croaked. "Catch it! There it goes! Kill it! Kill! Kill!"

We were close up to the stones now. The horrid feathery presences of the crows were all around, brushing against us; I felt a sharp bill stab at my back and beside me I heard Ned snort, "Ouch! Keep off, you nasty beggar."

The lightning flashed again. We were ready for it this time, looking in the direction from which we had last heard

Stanley's chilling howls and shrieks; there he was, on the ground this time, darting about here and there, keeping out of the way of the crows. And there, only a few yards away, was Pansy—curled into a small, terrified orange ball in the middle of a great flat stone slab. He darted towards her and we saw him grab hold of her at the same instant as the place was plunged once more into darkness.

Thunder rolled, drowning everything. Then the lightning shone again, twice, in two great white blinks; Stanley was coming towards us, half-dragging and half pushing Pansy. And the crows too had had time to see what was going on. They were massing all round, diving down at him, at us . . . Ned whinnied at him, "Wotcha, Stanley, old son! Nice work! This way."

"Yah!" shrieked Stanley. "Yah! Boo! Stupid birds! Ignorants! Loonies!" He took a flying leap on to Ned's back, with Pansy scrabbling after him. I could see them both, clinging on there while Ned plunged and shied about, trying to get away from the crows. The sky, I realised with horror, was beginning to get lighter; they could pick us out now, and were coming at us from all sides. The Major was hanging on to Ned's back, too, hurling insults at the crows, and Offa was circling overhead, making alarm calls and chuntering on about the hosts of darkness and the armies of evil. I felt another of those sharp beaks rip at my fur and thought, I don't see how we're going to get out of this.

A great wind seemed to sweep past overhead. I heard some of the crows calling out in fright. The wind came again. I glanced up and saw a brown shadow float across the circle. "You people having a spot of difficulty?" said a voice.

It was the eagle.

After that everything happened very fast. The eagle

128

circled up and then came dropping down like a stone, his great talons spread out; the crows began to scatter in panic. I shouted to the others to get away as fast as they could, and saw Ned charge out between two of the stones, with Freda close behind. The eagle rose, and came plummeting down again, with the crows spraying up around him in all directions, wailing to each other. Ned burst through the crowd of animals outside the stone circle, who were wandering around in a bemused state asking what had happened. I turned to look back, and saw the crows lift from the stones in a great flock and flap away into the brightening sky. The storm clouds were rolling off now towards the west, and there in the east, beyond the central stone of the circle, was the great red rim of the rising sun. Ned too paused for a moment, and Stanley, standing upright on his back, waved his hands at the sun and shouted to the animals, "There! Look, stupids!" The crows were streaming away towards the horizon now, shaggy shapes against the dawn sky. The stone circle was empty. On top of a low wall, a robin had begun to sing.

We stopped a mile or so away, and after a few moments the eagle joined us. He floated lazily down and sat on a tree-stump. "Awful lot of fuss and bother," he said. "What was all that about?"

We explained. The eagle made some contemptuous remarks about the undistinguished people you got around these parts and said graciously, in answer to our thanks, that he was always glad to lend a hand to old friends. He was on his way to Wales, he explained, and had been blown off-course by the storm. "Bit of a nuisance. But I suppose it's an ill wind etcetera . . . Been keeping fit, have you?" He glanced at Stanley and went on, "Your little friend seemed to be making himself quite useful in that business back there."

Stanley looked down at the ground modestly.

"Damn fine scrap," said the Major with enthusiasm. "Nothing like a good scrap."

The eagle looked at him and then at the rest of us and said, "What's that?"

I explained that the Major was a parrot.

"Much too ornate," said the eagle. "Awfully bad taste. Not British, I imagine."

The Major was looking deeply offended so I changed the subject by asking the eagle if he meant to stay long in Wales. A far-away look came into his glaring eye. "Matter of fact," he said, "one's been toying with the idea of a change of scene. Fresh fields and pastures new, you know. Relative of mine came across this place America recently— discovered it by chance. One feels the restrictions a bit, from time to time, in this country. Ever been to America?"

We said we hadn't. Freda asked what it was. The eagle looked supercilious and said that it was beyond where the sun sets and if you went on for long enough across the water you got there. "Awful lot of opportunities, I'm told. For the go-ahead sort of bird. By the way," he added, "did you ever get to that place you were looking for, London?"

We said we were still looking, and now that we'd got Pansy back again we'd pick up QV 66 at Oxford and get on with it.

"Oxford?" said the eagle thoughtfully. "Place with a river going through it?"

I said, "That's right."

"Glad you mentioned that. I can put you on your way in that case. That river goes to London—I came across it the other day, as it happens, London, that is. Came down to have a look at a possible roost—castle kind of place by a bridge, but it turned out to be not quite up to the mark, called The Tower or some such name. Anyway, one had a

130

look round while one was there—remarkably large city, you'll find it quite interesting. But later, when one was cruising at five thousand feet, one happened to notice that the river comes down from Oxford. Just thought I'd mention it. Stick to the river and you can't go wrong."

We thanked him profusely and said we hoped he'd be happy in America. The eagle invited us all to drop in sometime if we ever happened to be over that way, flapped his wings lazily and took off. We watched him lift up into the early morning sky and get gradually smaller and smaller. The Major, who was still in a huff, muttered about uppish fellows who didn't know how to be civil.

"There, now," said Freda soothingly, "we don't think you're ornate, we think you're very handsome." The Major preened himself, slightly mollified.

None of us, what with one thing and another, had had time to pay much attention to Pansy. She seemed, on the face of it, none the worse for her experiences, and was sitting in a patch of sunshine polishing her whiskers; she had grown quite a bit. I asked her what the balloon flight had been like. "Oh, that," said Pansy airily, "I'd almost forgotten. Rather frightening. Thank you for coming to look for me," she added, as an afterthought.

She had drifted, she told us, for quite a while in the basket, as the balloons became smaller and more shrivelled, until finally the basket got lodged in the branches of a tree and she was able to jump out. "Then what?" prompted Freda—Pansy was busy cleaning behind her left ear and seemed to have lost interest.

"Then I washed and tidied, of course," said Pansy. "I was looking awful." She began an intent inspection of her paws.

We did, eventually, manage to extract from her what had happened. She had wandered around for several days,

131

expecting that we might turn up at any moment, since she had no idea how far she had travelled. She even asked other animals if they had seen us and it was this, in the end, that attracted the attention of the crows. They must have been looking out for a likely creature to make the victim of their midsummer ceremony, and a small, distinctive cat that no one could remember seeing in the area before, without friends and relations, seemed to have been especially provided for the purpose. They had followed her around for several days before making a move. Pansy shuddered at the memory of that; wherever she went, she said, there seemed to be a still, black shape hunched on a wall or gate or tree nearby, until at last the day came when she woke from a snooze somewhere to find herself surrounded by them. Dozens of them, just sitting quietly around her, watching. She had made a dash for it, and was grabbed in a pair of steel claws. After that, she said, she couldn't really remember much until she found herself on the great slab in the middle of the stone circle, guarded by a ring of crows, with a murmuring of other animals coming from all around. She had had no idea of what was going to happen, except that she was a prisoner, and terrified, and that whatever the crows intended for her, it could not be anything pleasant.

"And then there was the storm, and then I saw Stanley . . ."

"And I rescued you," said Stanley.

I remembered something all of a sudden. I said, "Stanley, was it you making that peculiar noise? In the battle with the crows."

"Yes," said Stanley, "wasn't it interesting? I didn't know animals like me made that kind of noise. I was so angry and excited I just kind of opened my mouth and it came out. Shall I see if I can do it again?"

"No, thank you," said Freda hastily.

Stanley said dreamily, "It was the greatest battle there's ever been," and I must say that no one felt inclined to disagree with him. We spent the day resting quietly in the sunshine, and Stanley made up a poem—a long, elaborate poem—about what had happened, and in the evening he recited it to us, very dramatically with much gesture and pauses for effect and suspense, so that although we all knew what came next it became like the story of something that had happened to someone else. "Gracious!" Freda kept exclaiming, "No!" and "Just listen to that!" Needless to say Stanley emerged as the hero of the tale, but in the circumstances you could hardly grudge him that, and to give him credit the rest of us featured fairly magnificently as well. We all went to sleep feeling five times life-size.

We headed for Oxford as fast as we could. It was a tiresome journey, going back the way we had come, often by fields and hills and villages that we remembered from the outward journey. But it did mean that we were able to see how much the water had gone down. It was very rare, nowadays, to come across a flooded place, or even a stream that had overflowed its banks to occupy a valley. You could see, in these parts as elsewhere, that the water had once covered whole buildings in low places and a good deal of them in others, from the mess it had left behind and the tidemarks on the walls. But the landscape had, on the whole, gone back to pretty much what it must have been like in the first place, before the People left. We wondered, as we had done before, how long ago the floods had been, and why, and where the People went, and so forth. "Thousands of years ago," said Pansy. "Hundreds. Millions. Anyway, who cares? They were horrible, weren't they, the People, so what does it matter what happened to them?"

133

"Beefburgers . . ." said Freda, with a shudder. She often returns to that subject, and has drawn her own conclusions. "Sharp sticks for killing each other with. They had very nasty habits, didn't they? It's all for the best, that they disappeared. You don't get animals behaving like that."

I couldn't help reminding her of those dogs in Manchester. And the crows.

Then Stanley, who was in one of his Serious and Thoughtful moods, said he'd been doing some thinking about the People, and he'd decided they weren't entirely bad. In fact, he thought they might have been rather important ("Important!" said Ned, with a snort. "That lot! You must be joking!"). Yes, Stanley went on solemnly, they obviously had some pretty nasty habits, but there were all sorts of other things you had to take into account. All the things they made and invented — "Some of them must have been very, very clever, absolutely brilliant, actually I think I'm a little bit like some of them" — and those pictures in the Art Gallery in Manchester and the violin and all those books they wrote, and poems, and stories. They had nice feelings, he said, at least some of them did.

Freda said that was all very well, but it was no good having nice feelings and nasty habits.

We reached Oxford again at last and found QV 66 just where we had left it tied up at the bridge, untouched. Stanley was delighted to find all his precious things again and spent ages going through them to check that everything was there. Then, with the eagle's useful information in mind, we unhitched the boat and pointed it downstream to London: it seemed appropriate that it should carry us in style for the last stage of the voyage. We left Oxford on a bright sunny morning, moving fast downstream with the current. Stanley was sitting at the back, perched up on his seat, his box and the *Shorter Oxford English Dictionary* beside him, playing something loud and dramatic on the violin. We were all in high spirits, excited about what lay ahead.

10

In which we reach London and find out what Stanley is

The river was wide and fast and we made good progress. From time to time, though, we came to great barriers across the water, with passages at one side for boats to go through. The passages themselves were closed by gates so that on the first occasion we despaired and did not see how we could get QV 66 through until Stanley, after a great deal of concentration and a long headache, discovered that you could open the gates by turning a wheel beside them. It was a slow business, and meant that each time we came to one of the barriers it held us up for quite a while.

But we were getting nearer to London all the time. Offa, who flew around every now and then to inspect the road signs nearby, reported that the river did a good bit of twisting and turning, in the usual way of rivers, so that it was by no means the most direct route, but it was certainly the easiest, despite the barriers. And we all felt it somehow appropriate that the journey should end as it had begun, on board QV 66. And that the boat should be returned to its proper home. We wondered how it had ever got so far away in the first place. Freda supposed that it must have just drifted, when the floods began, or at some time since, but as Offa pointed out, it would have drifted in the opposite direction, the way the river was going. So Stanley made up a story about it, about some of the People being left behind and sailing off in it to try to find high ground on which to make a new home. "Nice People," he said, "not like the rest of them. Actually they took some animals with them, because they thought in this new place where they were going to start things again there ought to be animals, so they took one of each kind—no, two of each each kind—and there was this bird who flew on ahead, he was like Offa in fact, and . . ."

"Oh, don't be silly, Stanley," said Freda. "That's a stupid story, that couldn't happen." Offa, though, looked thoughtful and said he had a peculiar feeling he'd heard something like it before—or read it—long ago when he was young.

The nearer we got to London the more buildings there were. It was as though they had spread out and gobbled up the country. There were fewer and fewer animals around, too—plenty of small fry by way of birds, squirrels, cats, some dogs and so forth, but all the bigger things like cows and sheep had moved away, clearly. Since all this part had been under water the buildings were very dilapidated and smashed up and there wasn't much in them, except the high ones, so we didn't bother to do much exploring, but just moved on down the river. Ned and Freda, when they stayed on the banks, sometimes got left behind and we'd have to stop for them to catch up again.

There was less and less open space. At either side of the river were buildings as far as you could see, street upon street of houses and big factories from time to time. Offa reported that it was like that in all directions now.

"Then we're there?" said Freda. "This is London?"

The Major, who had been getting more and more excited at the prospect of re-visiting his old haunts, peered round and said that it didn't somehow look right to him. And then Offa pointed out that the bridge ahead was called Twickenham Bridge, and the road signs still talked of London. He was looking rather puzzled. I said, "What's up?"

"Nothing." He blinked and gave a nervous glance at the river. "Every fowl of the air, and everything that creepeth upon the earth . . . There's something peculiar in there." We all looked, but there was nothing to be seen. I said, "What sort of thing?"

Offa said evasively, "Hard to say. Think perhaps I imagined it. Hope so, anyway."

We drifted on, keeping close in to the bank, because Ned was on land, getting some exercise on a convenient track alongside the river. Freda was lying down in the middle of QV 66, chewing the cud and dozing. Pansy was sitting up in front, watching a sparrow that had been unwise enough to use the boat as a perch. Stanley, Offa and I were at the back. Stanley was steering, and giving us a running commentary on the various sights we were passing. "That very grand house is a palace where one of their kings lived," he said. "He was the king of this place Twickenham and he was a famous violin player, like me. He was king because he played the violin better than anyone else in the world. And that place over there is . . ." He stopped, with his mouth still open, staring at a muddy stretch of bank just ahead. "No!" he said faintly, and then, "Help!"

There was an animal on the mud. It was an animal so extraordinary that we simply gaped in amazement. It was enormous, bigger than a horse, with mud-coloured furless skin, and hugely fat. It had little short thick legs, and a great wide head topped with very small ears and eyes. It was slopping about in the mud, and as we watched it suddenly opened its mouth in a cavernous yawn, revealing a huge pink interior and rows of stubby teeth. Then it waddled down towards the water.

Freda said hysterically, "There aren't things like that! Someone made that up—it's not real!"

Stanley's eyes were nearly popping out of his head. The Major was shuffling up and down saying it was a rum do all right and he never saw such a thing in all his born days. "What is it?" said Pansy, in astonishment, forgetting the sparrow.

"It's a . . ." Stanley began. "Well, I'm pretty sure it's a . . . Actually I think in fact it's a . . . I don't know what it is," he finished lamely. And then, in sudden excitement he shouted, "Like me! Like we don't know what I am! There must be other animals that there's only one of!"

"Let's ask it what it is," I said, and at the same moment the animal slithered into the river and vanished. Moments later a smooth brown island with a pair of prick ears and two nostrils surfaced in midstream and drifted away out of sight.

"Well!" said Freda.

"Do you think it was fierce?" said Pansy uneasily.

We continued down the river in a state of considerable excitement, scouring the banks and the water for anything strange. There was nothing to be seen: just seagulls scavenging at the high-water mark and a few patrolling ducks.

The river was getting wider and wider. Here and there, stuck against the bridges or banks, there were smashed-up boats, many of them quite large. Once, we saw something very like QV 66, called HT 89. The buildings crowding the banks became more and more imposing: it was clear that we were getting to the centre of things. We cruised slowly past factories with gigantic chimneys, huge contraptions of wire and metal, great towering glass buildings with tier upon tier of windows. "That's the Great Palace of London," Stanley would say solemnly, and then, a few hundred yards later, as an even more striking building came in view, "no, I was wrong, actually *that* is . . ."

Offa had been chatting with some seagulls and came back to report that according to them the river began after a while to get even wider still, and quite soon it went into the sea. They said, apparently, that we were near a bridge with some great buildings beside it that was just about the middle of the city. He had asked them, also, about the brown animal, but at that they had become a little evasive. All they would say was that you saw some odd people around, from time to time. Stanley said impatiently, "Did they say if there's anyone like me?"

Offa hesitated. "I did ask," he said, "and they just laughed, as though I'd said something very stupid. Just laughed and flew off."

It had been noticeable, for some time, that what birds and animals there were around did not stare at Stanley in the usual way. I had not remarked on this to him, since I didn't quite know what to make of it anyway, and Stanley had not noticed since he was too busy pointing out the sights to everyone.

When, before long, we arrived at the bridge and the great buildings to which the seagulls had referred, it was impossible to feel anything but overawed. They were enormous; we felt very small and insignificant. The Major was scurrying up and down pointing things out and having hazy recollections that he had been here before. Stanley steered the boat towards a flight of steps, jumped on to them, and scampered ashore.

141

The rest of us disembarked after him, and stared round. QV 66, somewhat the worse for wear, scratched and battered, but still leering boldly ahead with the two eyes that Stanley had painted on it back in Warwick, bumped against the steps. Stanley tied the rope to an iron ring and said, "Of course, if we decide to stay here I shall need my tools. And the violin. And the books. You wouldn't mind carrying them, would you, Ned?"

"Yes," said Ned sourly, "I would."

Stanley was about to raise objections, so I cut in hastily and pointed out that we could always come back for anything we wanted. "Oh, all right," said Stanley with a sigh. "Come on, then."

"Where are we going now?" said Pansy.

That was a problem. There were a lot of road signs around still, though many of them were unreadable from having been underneath mud and water. They pointed in all directions, talking of places called Kensington, Piccadilly, or The City. We wandered about, dazed by the size of everything. There was a vast cathedral; Offa flew all around it, inspecting every nook and cranny, moaning happily. Stanley explored the great building beside the river. It had an enormous room, he said, bigger than anything you ever saw, with rows and rows of seats in banks. "I think it's another of those places where they pretended to be People they weren't really, and other People sat and watched," he explained. He was very excited and stimulated by everything.

We wandered around for hours, up great wide streets, past buildings that seemed to grow larger all the time, over grassy places with trees where Freda and Ned would insist on stopping for a rest and a graze. The whole place was a dreadful mess, littered with rubbish and driftwood and broken glass and thousands of cars all rusted and smashed up by the water. Obviously the floods had not long gone down, here. There weren't many animals about, but plenty of birds.

From time to time we came across figures of People made in stone or metal, frequently sitting astride horses. "You wouldn't have caught me putting up with that," snorted Ned. "Not flipping likely!" Sometimes the figures had names and writing underneath: King This and Queen That, and once one called General Somebody, which got the Major very interested. He clambered all over him, peering at his clothes and his face and muttering about regiments and battalions and parades.

There was so much to distract us that we frequently became confused and found we had been in a circle, returning to places we had visited before. "Zoo," Stanley kept saying, remembering that picture in Carlisle Station, at the beginning of the journey, so long ago, as it now seemed. "London Zoo, that's what we're looking for," but then he would rush off to explore some other interesting place, and forget about it. As usual he was full of explanations for everything. "This is a special place for telling stories in," he announced, in front of a huge round building with a notice outside saying Royal Albert Hall. "There was this great King called Albert Hall who was better at telling stories than anyone else, which is why he was made King, and he used to tell his stories to thousands of People in here, that's why it's got so many seats inside. And once," he went on, his eye caught by writing scrawled in big letters on some boarding outside—SPURS RULE O.K.?— "once he had a terrible battle with this person called Spurs who came and said he was even better at telling stories and they fought for three days and three nights on that bit of grass there on the other side of the road and at the end King Albert Hall threw this Spurs person into that lake there and . . ."

"Belt up, Stanley," said Ned with a yawn. "Come on . . ."

We wandered off again, with Stanley skipping on ahead, explaining and commenting, shinning up trees and buildings, disappearing and reappearing half a street away.

Offa came flying down to say that he had found what was quite definitely the most important church in these parts. "The halls of Zion. Funny, though, it's not the usual thing inside, at all. Got lots of rooms, full of glass boxes—you can see through the windows."

The building, when we reached it, had a great flight of steps up to a wide church-like door. There was a notice outside that said BRITISH MUSEUM (NATURAL HISTORY SECTION). Stanley went bustling up the steps. Freda, who had spotted some grass, said, "I'm staying out here, if you don't mind." I was just about to follow Stanley inside when he came bolting out again. I said, "Whatever's the matter?"

Stanley subsided in a heap on the bottom step. He was utterly speechless. Once or twice he gasped and spluttered and tried to say something, and then just waved helplessly towards the doorway again. "Brace up, Stanley, old son," said Ned, "get a hold of yourslf."

"In there . . ." said Stanley at last. "Great enormous somethings . . . Gigantic impossible not real . . . I think," he ended up solemnly, "I'm having an awful dream."

We trooped up the steps, Stanley last. "It's not that I'm *afraid* or anything," he was saying, "nothing like that, of course. Just it's your turn really to have first look. I just thought you'd like to see *first*, that's all."

We went in. There was a great room, reaching up to a high ceiling, just like a church or cathedral, as Offa had said. And at the end stairs both sides going up to another floor, with galleries round, and in the middle of the huge room, confronting us . . .

"No!" shrieked Freda. "Help! Let me get out of here!"

I said, "Hang on—they're not alive, whatever they are. They don't move."

They were animals. They were colossal. They towered above us, grey and immense and unbelievable. Gingerly, we edged nearer.

"They made them of animals too," said Stanley in awe, "like they did of themselves. Pretend ones." We read the printed label at the creature's feet: "African Elephant". "There can't have *been* things like that," said Freda. "I mean, there just can't have been."

Ned had clumped round to look at more huge creatures on the other side of the stand. "Here," he said suddenly, "take a look at this!"

It was a great brown animal just like the one we had seen on the banks of the river that morning: "Hippopotamus", said the label. Freda was stamping about in a fuss saying, "Then there *are*! That proves it! I don't like the look of them, either!"

The rest of us were more interested than alarmed. Stanley was rushing around chattering and exclaiming. There were glass cases against the walls full of the most bewildering things: bones and stones and more imitation animals, some believable and some not, pictures and writing and more bones.

"What's it all for?" said Ned in astonishment.

"It's a place where they invented animals," Stanley was saying. "They had ideas for new animals and put them together and then if they thought they were good ones they made lots but if they didn't work they just . . ."

"Stanley!" yelled Pansy. "Come here! Quick!"

She had gone up the stairs on to the gallery above. We could see her face peering out excitedly from between two glass cases. We hurried to join her. "There!" she was saying. "And there! And another one there! *Look*, Stanley!"

There were case after case of them; they clung realistically to dead tree branches, or squatted on their haunches

145

staring out with round glass eyes, or hung upside down by their tails. "Humboldt's Woolly Monkey", said the labels. "Brown Capuchin Monkey." "Red Howler." "Black and White Colobus Monkey." "Baboon." "South American Spider Monkey."

For a moment or two nobody said a word. Then at last Freda sighed. "Well, Stanley, now we know what you are, anyway. We do know that, at least."

Stanley sat and stared at the glass cases. He looked both solemn and sorrowful. Once Ned said, "Very nice too, Stanley, old son. Very well constructed, some of them. Got variety. Imagination."

"Do you mind being quiet?" said Stanley, in a stiff, dignified voice. "I'd rather not talk just at the moment."

After a long time he got up and slowly inspected all the cases in turn.

146

"That one's most like you," said Pansy cautiously. "At least no, I think perhaps *that* is."

Stanley scrutinised each case. Then he turned mournful black eyes upon us and said, "Well, I suppose that's it?"

I said, "Not necessarily. After all, we saw one of those hippo-what's-it things this morning. Just because there don't seem to be any more monkeys around doesn't mean . . ."

"P'raps they all went away," Freda suggested. "Or maybe you're a new kind."

Stanley gave her a look of tired resignation. "This," he said, waving his hand around at the glass cases, "is a place for inventing animals. Some of them worked and some of them didn't. I take it . . ." He gestured towards the monkeys. "I take it that these didn't. They're here to remind you not to try that kind of thing again."

"Then how come there's you?" said Ned.

Nobody could answer that, not even Stanley. Indeed, he cheered up a bit and admitted that there did seem to be a mystery somewhere. Ned, who had wandered away up the gallery, called that there was a relation of Freda's on show. In one of the cases stood a huge shaggy creature labelled North American Bison. Freda said coldly that it was an extremely distant relation, as far as she was concerned.

We roamed from room to room, from glass case to glass case, calling out to each other at each new discovery. "Now I've seen everything!" said Ned, in front of an amazing creature covered all over with long black and white spines. "Porcupine, indeed! I ask you! What's the point of a thing like that?"

"General similarity to hedgehogs?" suggested the Major.

"What about this, then?" said Freda, staring with fascinated disgust at something called a Giant Anteater.

"I mean, I think that's just ridiculous. If I looked like that I'd feel *embarrassed*." She swung her horns about petulantly. As you may have gathered, Freda does not at all care for things being unusual or out-of-the-ordinary. She takes it as a personal offence.

And if you felt like that there was a great deal to take offence at in that place. There were animals so peculiar, with such odd arrangements by way of feet, tails, claws, teeth, scales, fur and what-have-you that all we could do was gape and exclaim. There were animals larger than we would have thought possible; there were birds of every size, shape and colour (including some like the Major himself, which made us all even more thoughtful about the whole business); there were fish and insects of such amazing appearance that we stared in disbelief. Stanley vanished for a long time and came bounding back to take us to a room he had discovered downstairs where there were only the bones of animals—bones so immense that the animal skeletons, bigger even than the African Elephant, towered above us. Like the other things in that part of the building, the water had washed around them a bit but left most of them undamaged. Freda, staring up at something called Diplodocus, shuddered. "That's not funny," she said. "That's not even ridiculous. That's downright nasty."

Stanley had become very thoughtful. He squatted in front of one thing after another, his face wrinkled up in perplexity. He stared at cases full of nothing but stones shaped like snails, and cases full of bones and teeth and claws, with pictures of animals even more improbable than those that could be seen. When anyone spoke to him he snapped that he was having a headache and would we please leave him alone. Finally he announced that he had decided that this wasn't, after all, a place for inventing animals, but a place for making lists of them.

"Lists?" said Freda. "What did they want to do that for?"

"So that you could know exactly what there was," said Stanley impatiently. "Or what there had been. All this," he flung his arms out to take in the great stone-floored rooms, the glass cases, the multitude of creatures, "all this is everything there's ever been. Animals and things." He looked very solemn and serious. "I think it's the most important place we've ever discovered."

"Very impressive," agreed the Major. "Damn fine job."

Offa, who had found a convenient roost in the rib-cage of an immense skeleton called Tyrannosaurus Rex, said that the book he had read in Lichfield Cathedral when he was young told you all about that. "Let there be a firmament," he droned. "Let the waters bring forth abundantly the moving creature that hath life. It took seven days, apparently."

Stanley frowned. "I don't think you could have done all that in seven days. They must have got it wrong. But you don't understand," he went on impatiently, "you haven't got the point. The question is: which am I?"

"You're a monkey," said Pansy. "Easy." She sat on top of a marble pillar, grooming herself, and glancing now and then with an envious look at a startlingly striped cat-like creature in a glass case. "I wish my whiskers were a bit longer," she said. "I wish I was black and white."

"Not which *kind* of animal, am I," said Stanley. "Am I one that still exists or one that doesn't?"

"I'd say you exist all right, mate," said Ned. Stanley gave him a freezing look.

We were all somewhat exhausted by the day's adventures. Freda said if she didn't get off those stone floors soon and on to a nice bit of grass, there'd be trouble. With some difficulty, we persuaded Stanley to leave the museum and come with us. He was still dashing around peering into cases and going on to us about how we didn't understand how important all this was, and how would *we* like it if we didn't know whether or not we were the only monkey not inside a glass case? The Major pointed out that he had something of the same problem, himself, but wasn't making so much fuss about it. Stanley sniffed and said some people had extremely strong feelings, and there wasn't anything they could do about it. We dragged him out at last, grumbling, as darkness was falling on the deserted, rubbish-littered streets, and headed for a nearby open space with some trees, that we had noticed before. It seemed as good a place as any in which to spend the night.

11

In which Stanley meets his friends and relations, and the voyage ends, though perhaps not in quite the way that might have been expected

The next morning we set off early on another journey of exploration. Both Ned and Freda were complaining about the hardness of the streets and would have liked to spend the day grazing, but Stanley would have none of that. "Here we are," he said dramatically, "at the end of this important journey I've let you come with me on, and all you want to do is eat grass. You've got no sense of occasion, that's your trouble. Anyway"—with his most mournful and pathetic expression—"I thought we were still looking for my friends and relations?"

I don't think that any of us really believed any more that we were going to find any, but we hadn't the heart to tell him, so we trudged on up and down streets, across open spaces, into buildings and out of them again. There was so much that was surprising and interesting that even Freda perked up a bit. Stanley and I, investigating those entrances called Underground, discovered the People's system of tunnels and staircases and railways under the city. "This," said Stanley, scurrying up and down flights of stairs, "is where they went at night because they were frightened of the dark, you see. No, they didn't—it's that they couldn't bear getting wet when it rained so when the weather was bad they came down here to travel about and keep dry. I suppose it goes on for ever—you could go anywhere." It was still flooded down there, in most places, and dark and smelly, so we came out again.

We stopped to rest for a while in a large open space with a great many pigeons, and a high pillar with a figure on it in the middle. There were stone figures of strange, enormous animals at the four corners of the place, sitting with their front paws stretched out and their great bushy stone heads staring at the empty streets and buildings. "They were for a kind of magic," explained Stanley in awed tones. "The People used to come here when they were in trouble and have a special ceremony and ask those animals what they ought to do, and they sang beautiful songs to them and played them very special music, like I do with my violin—or at least like I used to when I still had it"—he glared at Ned—"and the stone animals used to come to life and start to talk in great deep voices . . ."

"Stanley," said Freda, bored, "you're making all that up, aren't you?"

"Yes," said Stanley after a moment. He climbed up on one of the animals and pranced around for a while, and then came down again and fidgeted about, pulling up the grass that was growing up between the paving stones. "I wonder what the People were like," he said suddenly.

"Who cares?" said Ned with a yawn. "Here, just shift off that dandelion, there's a good fellow. Thanks."

"Horrible, I should think," said Pansy. "And there were too many of them. And they were all exactly alike—you've only got to look at their pictures." She sprawled out in the sunshine, purring.

"They might not have been," said Stanley. "They might

have been all different, like us. Like you're not like Freda and I'm not like you . . ."

"Thank goodness," said Pansy.

". . . and I'm not like anything else at all," he ended, with a dignified and reproachful look.

"Not all of us," I said, feeling a bit irritated with him, "would want a long skinny tail."

"I was talking," said Stanley, "about one's personality, not one's tail."

He gave an ostentatious sigh and I could see we were in for a long session of Stanley being Misunderstood, when all of a sudden Offa, from his perch on an iron railing, said, "Eh! What's that, then? Up at the top of those steps there . . ."

There was a very large building at one side of the square, an imposing place with one of those fronts made of pillars, and flights of steps leading up to them. At the top of the steps, at one side, something was moving. Some kind of cart, it seemed to be. A small, rather battered wooden cart. It came shunting out of the building, and then stopped at the steps. Behind it, something brown and furry moved in the shadow of the porch.

"Better have a dekko," said Ned. We walked cautiously across the road, watching.

The cart jittered at the top of the steps, and then withdrew again. From behind it a voice said distinctly, "Bother!"

The cart lurched and tipped again, and out of the shadows stepped a brown monkey. He was a little larger than Stanley. He surveyed the cart, which seemed to be loaded with something, looked down the flight of steps, saw us, and said, "Would you people care to give me a hand?" He spoke rather peevishly, and immediately turned his back on us again and set to rearranging his load.

153

We climbed the steps. "They tell you to redecorate the conference room," the monkey was grumbling. "Just get on with it, they say. Never give a thought to the hows and wherefores. Expect you to do all the deliveries on your tod." He glanced at Stanley. "Here, just take one side, would you, and we can get it down the steps."

The cart, I now saw, was full of pictures of People. Large, painted ones like the ones we saw in Manchester, with heavy gold frames. The one on top was of a Person: a gold label underneath said, "Self-portrait aged 63 by Rembrandt."

Stanley said, in strangled tones, "Hello."

"Hello," said the monkey casually. "Bit far afield, aren't you?" Then he looked at Stanley more attentively and added, "I haven't seen you before."

I could see that things really weren't going very well, from Stanley's point of view. I said to the monkey, "Our friend Stanley has travelled from a very long way away to find his friends and relations. It's the first time he's ever seen one of you."

Stanley said grandly, "This is the most important moment of my life." They had got the cart to the bottom of the steps by now and the monkey was busy rearranging his load of pictures. A different one had now appeared on top— two People looking tired, labelled "Venus and Mars, by Botticelli"—which he poked petulantly. "Get nice big ones, they tell me, never give a thought to the weight." He eyed Stanley and said, "Well, you'd better come along and register as a new admission, I suppose. There was another of you not so long ago—a colobus from Bristol or some such place. They'll have to set up a committee to consider your case, of course, but I daresay they'll give you temporary residence until the decision comes through. Come on—we'd better get moving if we're getting in before sunset."

154

Stanley was in such a state of agitation that we thought for a moment that he was going to go off with the other monkey, just like that. He was gazing at him in admiration saying "Yes" and "No" and "Exactly" every time he spoke. "Cheerio, then, Stanley," said Ned. "All the best."

"What do you mean?" said Stanley indignantly. "Aren't you coming too?"

"Doubt if that'll be possible," said the monkey. "Regulations, you know. Other species not usually admitted, except former residents."

"They're my friends," said Stanley, a hint of his usual spirit returning. "Of course they must come."

"Suit yourself," said the monkey. "Have to sort it out when you get there."

So off we trundled once more, through the streets, with Stanley and the monkey pushing and pulling the cart full of pictures, assisted eventually by Ned when we managed to find a length of rope with which to hitch it to him. The monkey's name, it appeared, was Friday. He was not, one had to admit, a very stimulating companion. He grumbled a great deal and explained nothing he said, as though he expected us to know all about everything. Neither did he show the slightest curiosity in us. He stumped across London complaining about how "they" chivvied him around and expected miracles and never came up with so much as a thank you. At one point he decided to lighten the load in the cart by removing a picture—a large one of some very bad weather called "View of Margate, by J. M. W. Turner"—and throwing it down an entrance to the Underground. "They're never going to know, are they?" he said. "So long as they've got the coverage they want. Six big ones, that's what they said, and that's what they're getting. And I'm applying for a rest day after this lot, I can tell you, and if there's questions asked I shall put it to them fair and square, now look, I shall say . . ."

Even Stanley began to look a bit bored. I asked the monkey who "they" were.

"Well, it's them, isn't it?" he said impatiently. "And another thing—I'm not standing for any more of this fetching and carrying for the wombats. Just shift those stones over there; just move that pile of earth. No, I'm going to say, straight out, just like that, no. You can ask so much and no more. I've got my rights, same as anyone else . . ." He droned on, interrupted now and then by Stanley who is never very good at just listening to people and was anxious to tell Friday the story of the voyage of QV 66. Friday paid very little attention. The more Stanley told the more he went on about his own affairs, with neither of them really listening to the other at all. It didn't seem to be developing into much of a relationship.

At last, after an interminable journey, just as it was getting dusk, we arrived. We had crossed an open space with a lot of trees, and had gone through a gap in some railings into a street, and there suddenly was an entrance saying Zoological Gardens, with a lot of rusty ironwork barring the way in, and a couple of cross-looking monkeys squatting at either side. "About time too," said one of them to Friday. "Any longer and I'd have reported you late in. What's this lot, then?"—with a wave at the rest of us.

Friday, still grumbling, explained. His voice had taken on a different tone, though—whining and placating—as though these other monkeys were more important than he was and he had to be careful of his position with them.

They turned their attention to us. There was a whispered consultation and then one of them said, rather grudgingly, that we'd better come in and find somewhere to settle down for the night. They did not seem particularly interested in Stanley. "Have to report for your admission interview tomorrow," one of them said to him. "It's against regulations, mind, letting your friends in like this—but I daresay nothing'll be said if they push off before too long tomorrow."

Stanley seemed stupefied again—as well he might. As soon as we got inside we saw that there were monkeys everywhere, of all different sizes, shapes and colours, bustling around the place.

And the place itself was very odd. There were buildings, but many of them were made just of iron bars, or wire mesh, though most of these were half broken down, or had open doors. And there were some strange animals around, apart from the monkeys—brilliantly coloured birds, small stout brown creatures hurrying here and there, peculiar kinds of sheep.

But we were too tired to take in very much. Friday, who had trundled his cart off to a big stone building some way away, came back and took us to some open-fronted sheds where, he said, we could spend the night. Someone would come to fetch us in the morning, he said, and tell Stanley what he had to do.

We slept, exhausted.

It was not, however, Friday who came to fetch us, but a different monkey. He came hurrying along soon after we had woken and were still trying to adjust ourselves to these odd surroundings. He carried a sheaf of papers and was shuffling through them as he went, frowning and muttering to himself. When he got to us he looked at Stanley and said, "New applicant? Name of Stanley? This way, please—introduction tour and registration. Hurry up, please." He threw a glance at the rest of us and said, "No objection to the rest of your party joining the tour before they leave. Always interested in good public relations."

We followed him. Now that it was broad daylight it was possible to get a better idea of the place. The main impression one got was of intense activity. There were animals scurrying around everywhere—mainly, as I have said, monkeys, but with a good deal else thrown in. The whole place was in a terrible mess, too. Most of the buildings were ramshackle and untidy—partly as a result of the floods but partly because of the piles of rubbish and things of the People's which had obviously been brought in by the monkeys and then discarded. Outside one building, pictures were stacked in rows, along with broken-down chairs and tables. There was litter of one kind or another all over the place. Freda, who is fussy about that kind of thing, and will only graze in a nice clean place, picked her way through it with an expression of disapproval.

We came to an open space pitted all over with holes and burrows. Some of the stout brown animals we had seen yesterday were scurrying about, digging frantically and apparently without purpose. They would scrabble feverishly, as though their lives depended on it, and then abandon that place and start again a little way away. One of them was burrowing straight down beside a brick wall. Another was energetically shifting stones from one hole into another. Friday, looking sullen, was heaving earth about in his cart. I asked our guide what the animals were.

"Wombats, of course," he said. "Earth Investigation Centre. They're finding out what's underneath the world for us. Doing a fine job. We provide the facilities and they get on with it."

"But they're all digging different holes," said Stanley. "And they never finish any of them. Why don't you tell them all to dig one *big* hole, all together, and then . . ."

"They're experts," said the monkey sternly. "No point

in bringing in experts and then interfering." He gave Stanley a sharp look. "If anyone was asking your opinion, which they weren't."

We continued. Our escort, it appeared, was called Henry. He did not grumble like Friday, but also talked at great length, and, equally, showed very little interest in Stanley or the rest of us. Once, he said to Freda, condescendingly, "Up from the country, are you?" Freda looked at him coldly, and did not reply.

We came to a kind of artificial mountain made of stone. There were a number of sheep-like creatures clambering around, and half-way up, a very large monkey of quite startling appearance. He had a long, thin face, parts of which were bright blue. The back end of him was scarlet. He was sitting quite still staring at the sky. Henry said, in a low and respectful tone, "You may look at the Mandrill, but you must on no account speak to him. Please keep very quiet."

"What's he doing?" said Stanley. He was beginning to look a little less awed and impressed; there was a faint scowl on his face.

"He's thinking, of course," said Henry.

"What's he thinking about?"

Henry gave an exasperated sigh. "He's not thinking *about* anything. He's just having thoughts. That's the most difficult kind of thinking of all."

"I do that," said Freda, "when I'm sitting in a field having a good chew. It's a nice, cloudy comfortable feeling."

Henry said stiffly, "I'm afraid you haven't quite grasped the situation. The Mandrill is better at thinking than anybody else in the world. He is famous for it. We all admire him enormously."

The Mandrill gave a sudden sigh and twitched one leg.

159

"There," Henry whispered, "I expect he's had a thought." He said to the Mandrill respectfully, "Was it an interesting one?"

The Mandrill looked down his nose at us and said, "It was rectangular, and a very pale green in colour." He closed his eyes and appeared to be going to sleep.

"Marvellous . . ." said Henry. "He'll have to rest for a long time now."

Stanley was muttering to himself. Something about *stupid* and *pointless* and when *I* think, I think *about* something. Fortunately Henry did not hear. He was hurrying off down some steps. We followed him. Outside the entrance to a building he stopped. "I'm just going to take you in to see the Diana monkeys," he said. "Not that I imagine you'd be billeted with them"—he gave Stanley a look of distaste—"but you might as well be introduced."

The building, inside, was startling. It was draped all over with lengths of brightly coloured material—taken, obviously, from the People's ruined houses. There were other things of the People's scattered around, too—pots made of china and glass, heaps of their clothes, strings of beads and shiny things, ornaments of one kind and another. There were a number of monkeys there—large, black and white ones—but in contrast to the bustle of the rest of the place they were all lounging around doing nothing in particular. Some of them were admiring themselves in mirrors; some were asleep; others were just chatting to each other or messing about with paints and brushes.

"They're amazingly artistic," said Henry. "They're not like the rest of us. They're terribly sensitive." (Stanley perked up at this and stared critically at the black and white monkeys.) "And they understand things we can't understand. So we just see that they have plenty to eat and drink so that they can get on with what they're doing."

One of the monkeys was making a very complicated

arrangement out of bits of twig and feathers and various rags and shreds of paper. "It's making a nest," said Freda with interest, "I expect it's going to have a baby."

Henry tutted irritably. "They don't do ordinary things like that," he said. "I've just told you. They aren't like us. Or at least when they do ordinary things it's quite different for them."

"Then what *is* it making?," said Ned suspiciously. "That doesn't look very artistic to me. How do we know it's artistic?"

"We can't," said Henry crossly. "Only they can know that. The rest of us are too ordinary. Anyway," he went on, going back to his stern and bossy manner, "visitors aren't allowed to pass comments."

Stanley sniffed loudly.

We left the Diana monkeys and followed Henry across an open space with trees where a lot of very thin elegant monkeys with immensely long arms were swinging energetically from branch to branch. "Gibbon stadium," said Henry. "Careful—better keep back. I expect the race is about to begin."

The gibbons hurled themselves wildly from tree to tree, with much howling and shrieking. Every now and then a couple of them would break off to have a short fight, and then, without it being apparent that anything had been settled, return to hurtling around the trees. At one point two of them fought so hard that they had to drop out altogether and retire to the ground to nurse their injuries, sulkily. "They're fighting about who's going fastest," explained Henry. "Awfully difficult for them to be sure, and it's terribly important. One of them can go faster than anything in the world and they have to find out which."

"Why?" said Stanley.

"They ought to go in a straight line," said Ned. "I know

all about that sort of thing. You all start in one place and go on till you get there. You see my ancestors . . .''

Henry glared at him and hurried on. When we caught up with him he was standing beside an enclosure fenced off with an iron railing. In the middle of it was an island of earth with a single tree and underneath the tree was a large fat monkey with straggly reddish fur and a wrinkled face. He was squatting on an enormous pile of books. Henry said crossly, ''I was going to introduce you to the Orang-utan. Sometimes he can find a moment to have a word with visitors. But you're being so awkward that I shan't. And anyway we'll be late for the committee if we don't get on. You can just look at him.''

The Orang wore a pair of the People's spectacles without any glass in them. He was reading intently, and as we watched he closed the book and dropped it on to the pile beneath him. He climbed up on to it and sat down again and at once a small brown monkey handed him another book from a wheelbarrow stacked full of them. He began to read again, with an expression of weary suffering.

''He's reading all the books in the world,'' said Henry. ''Then he'll know more than anyone else has ever known before and we shall all respect him tremendously. Sssh!'' he added sternly. ''We'd better not interrupt.''

The Orang yawned and scratched his stomach and turned over a page of the book, which was called *Advanced Electronic Engineering*. He was sitting on *A Short History of Europe* and leaning against a backrest composed of *Mushroom Growing for Amateurs* and *Best Crime Stories*.

''I can read too,'' said Stanley loudly, ''but personally I think the point is . . .''

''Be quiet!'' snapped Henry. ''New admissions are not allowed to talk until screened by the committee. Come on.''

We had all been so absorbed and surprised by what we

163

had seen that there had been little time or opportunity for conversation or comment. Freda had a very pursed and disapproving expression and Ned gave a short snort every now and then. Pansy was fascinated by the monkeys and kept striking up brief friendships with the younger ones, which Henry put a stop to by sharply ordering them to get on with their work. "What work?" said Pansy sulkily. "Everybody's got work," said Henry. "That's what we're for."

"I'm not," said Pansy, but too quietly for him to hear, "I'm for having a nice time and sitting in the sun."

I said to Stanley, "Well, Stanley, reckon you'll be all right here?" He was about to answer when there was a loud squawk from overhead and we looked up to see a whole line of parrots, some of them red and green, others red and grey like the Major, others blue and yellow, perched on a tree like a lot of extravagant flowers. The Major, who was riding on Ned's back, gave an excited cry of recognition, and began to ask them questions about their rank and regiment and one thing and another. But the response was a sad disappointment. The birds screamed back at him all together, but what they said was unintelligible, except, apparently, to the Major, who looked upset and did not pursue the matter. "What's wrong?" said Pansy. "Aren't they nice?" The Major shook his head sadly and said that they were a very ungentlemanly kind of bird and he didn't care for that sort of language, not in the presence of ladies. He anchored himself to Ned's mane more firmly, blinking and muttering to himself.

"Laboratories," announced Henry. "Kindly don't touch anything." He led us into a long low brick shed. Outside, there was a notice on a piece of board, crudely printed in red paint, which said GRATE SIENCE DISCOVERYS DONE HERE SSSH! BRING YOR OWN BUKKIT NO PINCHING

164

ANYWUN ELSE'S EXPERRYMENTS CANTEEN OPEN ALL DAY CHIMPS ONLY.

There were a lot of large black monkeys inside, all intently busy on what they were doing. Some of them were pouring stuff out of bottles into buckets and carefully stirring the ensuing mixture; others were at work with glass tubes and jars, blowing and measuring and mixing; others were crouched over long benches with tools and heaps of bits and pieces of metal, cutting and bending and constructing. There was a great deal of noise and chatter. Every now and then one of them would give a whoop of excitement and all the others would gather round and jump up and down cheering and applauding.

"Chimps," said Henry. "They're awfully clever."

The chimp nearest to us was squatting in front of a bucket. It poured some paint into the bucket from a tin marked Dulux Super-Gloss, added a handful of dust and some dead leaves, pondered a moment or two and tipped in the contents of a bottle labelled Whitbread's Pale Ale. Then it stirred the mixture feverishly. When the brown sludge had settled it peered into the bucket and said with satisfaction, "Coming on nicely, I think."

Stanley said, "What are you doing?"

"I'm inventing something, aren't I?"

"Inventing what?"

"How can I know?" said the chimp impatiently. "Until I have. It'll be a surprise, won't it? Then if it's good I'll be famous."

Stanley said to no one in particular, "Once a long time ago I invented wheels and put them on QV 66 and another time I invented flying and . . ." I frowned at him. Henry was moving away down the shed and beckoning to us to follow him.

Three chimps were busy with a great heap of rusty iron

165

and some tools. They were building some kind of contraption from lengths of iron, fixing one bit to another in a disorganised way so that the object grew in all directions like some kind of unwieldy metal spider. One of them dropped a hammer on to its foot and immediately blamed another; a squabble broke out during which some bits fell off their construction. Stanley watched smugly.

Pansy said, "Is it going to be beautiful, that thing you're making?"

"What's beautiful?" said the chimp. He scrabbled around in the pile of metal, found a length of rubber pipe and looked at it thoughtfully.

"Huh . . ." said Stanley.

We joined Henry outside the shed. "That's the end of the introduction tour," he said. "Say thank you. Now it's time for your admission interview and registration. Come along."

Stanley was wearing his most obstinate and rebellious expression. I said, hastily before he could do anything tactless, "You haven't told us who he's got to see." —

"Or who you are," said Pansy ("except a bossy-boots," she added in an undertone).

Henry shook his head impatiently. "Really! Some people! Us, of course. We run everything, don't we? We decide what's going to be done and what isn't going to be done and how it ought to be done and when we're going to do it and . . ."

"Why?" said Stanley.

"Because we're more important than anyone else," said Henry. "Goodness, how stupid you are. I should have thought that was obvious. Do hurry up—we're late as it is."

He led us into a large building. The lettering on the notice beside it which said ELEPHANT HOUSE had been crossed out and the word GOVERNMENT painted over in red.

("What happened to the elephants?" said Freda, a touch nervously. "They went, a long time ago," said Henry, "along with the lions and the leopards and the giraffes and most of the bigger stuff—just as well, one couldn't always keep them under control.") From within there came a confused clacking noise.

There were monkeys—middle-sized brown monkeys like Henry himself—everywhere. A great many of them were banging away on battered typewriters. "They're getting the Minutes ready," explained Henry. "The Minutes and the Memoranda and the Reports and the Statements and everything." One small monkey was completely wreathed in lengths of red and black ribbon; he struggled frantically, becoming more and more entangled. "Poor fellow," said Henry, "he's got tied up with the Agenda. That happens."

I looked over the shoulder of the nearest typing monkey. QWERTY&£@! said the sheet of paper in front of him. PARAGARPH 5 SECTION 8 REGULATIONS AND INSTRUCTIONS BOTHER MADE A MISTAKE AGAIN BY ORDER AND AUTHORITY OF 23456789 DISREGARD ALL PREVIOUS ?!UIOP GOT PINS AND NEEDLES IN MY LEG.

At the far end of the building a very large monkey was sitting up on top of a pile of wooden crates sorting through a heap of papers. He seemed to be in a state of great agitation. Every now and then he would wave one of the papers in the air and other monkeys would come rushing up and take it from him and dash off with it. Then he would immediately howl at them to come back again, snatching away the paper and giving them another one instead. What happened to the bits of paper was not clear.

"He's making decisions," said Henry. "Terribly important job."

At the other side of the building another large monkey was sitting on top of an iron railing talking loudly and waving his arms about. It was not possible to hear what he said and nobody seemed to be listening anyway. "He's making the Speech for the Day," said Henry.

A monkey came bustling up to us. "This the new entrant?" he said. "The committee are waiting." He looked at the rest of us and said, "No visitors."

"They're my friends," said Stanley aggressively.

"Friends aren't in the regulations."

"Then the regulations are stupid," said Stanley. There was a buzz of disapproval from some of the typing monkeys, who clacked away even more feverishly. Some of them, I noticed, hadn't any paper in their typewriters. One of them was using a cabbage leaf. "Oh, all right," said Henry petulantly. "You'd better all come along, then. I've never known such a tiresome lot."

The committee was sitting on a bench in a row. There were five of them. The one in the middle wore a hat made out of a newspaper and a necklace of shiny stones. Without looking up, he droned, "Session forty-eight insofar as you the undersigned did conspire to contravene the motor vehicle registration act subject to and abiding by the aforementioned . . ."

"Excuse me, sir," said Henry respectfully. "New admission for screening. That's the Chairman," he added in an undertone.

The Chairman looked up. "No horses," he said. "No cows. No dogs. No cats. No more parrots or pigeons."

"And no Stanleys either," said Stanley loudly. Everybody stared at him, including Ned, Freda, Pansy, Offa, the Major and myself.

"Be quiet!" said Henry.

"I won't!" said Stanley.

"You're behaving very badly," said the Chairman. "If you're not careful we won't let you come here."

Stanley said, "I don't want to come here."

There were exclamations from all sides—"Shocking! How disgraceful! What impertinence!"

"You've got to come here," said the Chairman. "You're a monkey, aren't you? All monkeys come here."

"What does he think he is, then?" grumbled someone.

Stanley climbed up on to an iron railing and shouted, "What I think I am is ME and even if I know *what* I am now that doesn't make me like the rest of you and as a matter of fact I think the rest of you are just a lot of sillies, you're even stupider than I am sometimes . . ." He paused for breath and Ned muttered, "Steady on, Stanley old son . . ."

"What I think," Stanley went on dramatically, "is you do everything in a silly way here and why do you all stay here anyway?"

"We've always been here, haven't we?" said the Chairman in a tone of bewilderment. "Anyway where else is there?"

"There's lots of places," said Stanley. "There's everywhere. We've been to most of it, my friends and I. As it happens, we're famous for travelling and . . ."

"You're talking too much," shrieked Henry. "Nobody's allowed to talk as much as the Chairman!"

"Oh, phooey," said Stanley. He hopped down from the railing and said to the rest of us, "Come on. Let's go."

We trooped out through the monkeys, who were all chattering indignantly. One or two of them became aggressive and made attempts to stop us, but a few words from Ned and myself soon put an end to that. Henry dashed around us chattering with rage and shouting, "Come back! Come back at once! Nobody can leave without permission!"

169

"Make me!" taunted Stanley. "Go on! Tell your silly old committee to stop me!"

Our departure was noisy and conspicuous, but even so everyone seemed too preoccupied with what they were doing to pay much attention. The wombats glanced up for a moment and then turned back to their holes. Friday, tipping a barrow-load of earth on to the ground, stared at us and muttered something about always having said no good came of strangers. One or two passing monkeys looked curiously at us before hurrying off to their particular building or enclosure. Only Henry and a few of his friends trailed after us, commenting shrilly. Stanley, from time to time, commented back.

When we reached the exit the two monkeys on duty made a feeble attempt to stop us going. "Where's your pass?" they said. "Got to have a pass to go outside." "If you say so, mate," said Ned amiably. "If that's what makes you happy." And he shouldered his way through the gates, followed by the rest of us, leaving the monkeys gibbering angrily from within.

"And they went forth into the wilderness," said Offa with satisfaction. "And their enemies shall perish. Alleluia!"

We hurried away.

"Well," said Freda. "That's it, then. And now can we have a nice sit down somewhere, please."

There were things to be said, but none of us felt inclined to say them. "There you are then, Stanley," said Ned. "We found your friends and relations for you. We did that all right." And Stanley, who was behaving in a very subdued and unStanley-like manner, just nodded and pattered on ahead of us through the streets. He seemed to be deep in thought.

170

Once, Pansy said, "Just think, we might have been leaving Stanley there and going off without him."

"All set for a nice quiet life," said Freda, but not as though she really meant it. "*I* don't know," she went on, "we traipse half-way round the world to find his friends and relations and then when we find them it's no thank you. Never satisfied, that's his trouble."

Stanley turned round and said in aggrieved tones, "I heard that. You've hurt my feelings. I s'pose you wish I *had* stayed with them."

"Oh, I dunno, old son," said Ned cheerfully. "Reckon we're lumbered with you now." And Stanley's feelings, as on so many other occasions, did not stay hurt for long. Presently he began to caper on ahead instead of pattering, bouncing off every now and then for a quick exploration down a side-street or into a building. Eventually, we lost him altogether, and Freda, who was becoming more and more petulant about the state of her feet, sat down in the grassy middle of a square and said she was not going any further. And then, just as we were all about to settle down with her, Stanley reappeared. "Come on," he said excitedly. "I've found it. It's still there."

"What is?" said Freda suspiciously.

"The boat, of course," said Stanley. "QV 66. Come on, it's only just down at the end of this street."

Reluctantly, we went after him. We turned a corner and there was the river again, wide and full and glittering in the sunshine. And there, wedged up on a mudbank against a tidemark of rubbish, was the boat. And Stanley. And Stanley's box of precious things. He waved happily.

"The violin's all right," he said. "One or two of my tools have gone but otherwise everything's here. What we'll need," he went on busily, "is some food. Supplies and things, just for a bit, because of course we don't know how long it goes on for. Offa could fly on and have a look, I

suppose, but all the same we'd better load up with some
nuts and things in case I get hungry. And hay," he added,
with a quick glance at Ned and Freda.

"Stanley," I said, "what exactly are you on about?"

"Well, out there, of course," he said in surprise, waving
a thin hairy arm at the river. "Where it goes to. All that
water those birds said there is. What's on the other side
of it. I mean, you can't just sit about, can you? You've got
to find out about things."

Freda said she'd done about enough finding out for the
moment.

172

"You'll enjoy it once we get started," said Stanley cosily. "You'll see. It'll be very interesting and exciting, just like this voyage has been. After all, we're experts now, aren't we, about voyages, now that we've found London and we've found out what I am, so it would be silly not to do it again and see what else we can find. Come on." He hopped up on to his bicycle seat, tipped some rainwater out of his box, rearranged the *Shorter Oxford English Dictionary* and stowed the violin beside it. "Come on," he said. "There's this story I've just made up that I'm going to tell you about a famous Person who was better than anyone else at travelling and finding out about things—he was a bit like me—and he had these friends who always went everywhere with him and one day . . ."

We looked at each other. Freda heaved a sigh, I think. We climbed on board QV 66.

Other Classic titles available in
Mammoth:

Nina Beachcroft

A VISIT TO FOLLY CASTLE

Emma Jones is fascinated by the deserted Folly
Castle.

Folly Castle has been empty for years when the
eccentric Spellman family move in. Emma Jones
meets Sandra Spellman by accident when she
finds a message in a bottle – on dry land! Emma is
fascinated by this raven-haired stranger but she
doesn't realise what harm the mysterious Sandra
will cause...

Nina Beachcroft

WELL MET BY WITCHLIGHT

"Well met by witchlight" she found herself suddenly saying out loud. She could not be sleeping on such a night. It was a night for magic if ever a night was.

Mary is not your ordinary witch. Her powers have lain dormant for many years.

Can she triumph over the evil black witch? The malice, cruelty and uncanny evil of that face held them rooted; it was worse than they could have conceived possible...

Colin Dann

THE ANIMALS OF FARTHING WOOD

"We must face the facts" Toad ˋcried… "Farthing Wood is finished; in another couple of years it won't even exist. We must all find a *new* home. Now – before it's too late."

When men arrive with bulldozers in Farthing Wood, its animals and birds know that their world is doomed. The only chance for Badger, Toad, Kestrel and the others is a perilous cross-country trek towards a new life in a nature reserve. But not even Fox, their brave and intelligent leader, is prepared for all the dangers that lie ahead. And when disaster strikes the group, their new home seems an impossible dream…

Robert Louis Stevenson

TREASURE ISLAND

Into the 'Admiral Benbow' came the stranger. 'Call me captain,' he said. But for all his tough appearance, he was afraid of something.

Young Jim Hawkins, the landlord's son, discovers the seafarer's secret. He has a map – a map that guides the way to hidden treasure. Jim is determined to capture the map himself – but first he must outwit the sinister pirate, Pew, and then the flamboyant one-legged Long John Silver...

A piratical tale of high adventure and buried treasure.

Michael Scott

THE QUEST OF THE SONS

Found guilty of murdering evil Lord Cian, the three brave sons of Tuireann must make amends. Lugh exacts a terrible revenge for his father's death and demands that the brothers gather together the Seven Magical Treasures of Antiquity.

Brian, Urchar and Iurchar set out on their dangerous quest in the Navigator, a magical boat that travels as swiftly as the wind.

And, all the while, Lugh is watching them, determined to stop them succeeding...

Sir Arthur Conan Doyle

THE HOUND OF THE BASKERVILLES

"They all agreed that it was a huge creature, luminous, ghastly and spectral."

Sir Charles Baskerville dies mysteriously in the grounds of Baskerville Hall, a mansion isolated on Dartmoor. The whole district is gripped with terror – no-one will cross the moor at night. There is only one thing to be done – call in Sherlock Holmes.

Will the world's greatest detective be a match for the mysterious hell hound trapped on the moors?

Conan Doyle's most famous and intriguing case.

Mark Twain

THE ADVENTURES OF
HUCKLEBERRY FINN

On the run from his brutal father, Huck Finn sets off down the Mississippi River on a raft. With him is Jim, a runaway slave, and together they follow the river south. It's a voyage of discovery for both of them, as they meet up with two feuding families, an angry mob, and two tricksters who almost cost Huck and Jim their lives...

Michael Morpurgo

WHY THE WHALES CAME

'You keep away from the Birdman,' warned Gracie's father. 'Keep well clear of him, you hear me now?'

But Gracie and her friend Daniel discover that the Birdman isn't mad or dangerous as everyone says. Yet he does warn them to stay away from the abandoned Samson Island – he says it's cursed. And when the children are stranded on Samson by fog, Gracie returns home to learn of a tragic death. Could the Birdman be right?

On the day the whale is found stranded on the beach, the Birdman is forced to reveal his secret – or the cycle of disaster will begin all over again...

NOW A MAJOR FILM

Michael Morpurgo

WAR HORSE

It is 1914. In England, Albert is growing up on a Devon farm with a young horse he calls Joey. In Germany, Friedrich works in his butcher's shop. In France, Emilie and her brothers play in their orchard. But the clouds of war are on the horizon and great armies are gathering their strength. Soon they will all be drawn into the nightmare of battle.

This is the story of Joey and the people whose lives he touches, as they struggle for survival in the blasted wilderness of the Western Front.

A Selected List of Fiction from Mammoth

☐ 416 13972 8	**Why the Whales Came**	Michael Morpurgo	£2.50
☐ 7497 0034 3	**My Friend Walter**	Michael Morpurgo	£2.50
☐ 7497 0035 1	**The Animals of Farthing Wood**	Colin Dann	£2.99
☐ 7497 0136 6	**I Am David**	Anne Holm	£2.50
☐ 7497 0139 0	**Snow Spider**	Jenny Nimmo	£2.50
☐ 7497 0140 4	**Emlyn's Moon**	Jenny Nimmo	£2.25
☐ 7497 0344 X	**The Haunting**	Margaret Mahy	£2.25
☐ 416 96850 3	**Catalogue of the Universe**	Margaret Mahy	£1.95
☐ 7497 0051 3	**My Friend Flicka**	Mary O'Hara	£2.99
☐ 7497 0079 3	**Thunderhead**	Mary O'Hara	£2.99
☐ 7497 0219 2	**Green Grass of Wyoming**	Mary O'Hara	£2.99
☐ 416 13722 9	**Rival Games**	Michael Hardcastle	£1.99
☐ 416 13212 X	**Mascot**	Michael Hardcastle	£1.99
☐ 7497 0126 9	**Half a Team**	Michael Hardcastle	£1.99
☐ 416 08812 0	**The Whipping Boy**	Sid Fleischman	£1.99
☐ 7497 0033 5	**The Lives of Christopher Chant**	Diana Wynne-Jones	£2.50
☐ 7497 0164 1	**A Visit to Folly Castle**	Nina Beachcroft	£2.25